Mark Carew is the author of *The Book of Alexander*, and *Magnus,* both published by Salt. His short stories have appeared in print and online. He hosts the podcast *The Joy of Writing* where he discusses with fellow authors their books and the craft of writing.

BEYOND THE NORTH WIND

Mark Carew

ISBN-13: 9798651345823

Cover design by: Mark Carew
Image credit licensed for use from istockphotos.com
Library of Congress Control Number: 2018675309
Printed in the United States of America

The Good has nothing to do with purpose, indeed it excludes the idea of purpose. 'All is vanity' is the beginning and the end of ethics. The only genuine way to be good is to be good 'for nothing' in the midst of a scene where every 'natural' thing, including one's own mind, is subject to chance, that is, to necessity.

The Sovereignty of Good, Iris Murdoch

To all the dreamers still dreaming out there

CHAPTER 1

In the days that followed the captain's departure, I hid away on the farm run by his wife, Tone. A police helicopter picked its way in and out of the fjords, while I picked fruit with the other farmhands, nervous of the clatter of rotor blades overhead, wary at night of infra-red cameras. My fear subsided; it was not me they wanted. They were after the monster, the mountain man who had lit up the island of Svindel. He had terrorised five good, decent people from the university, threatening to burn them alive in their hut, but they had rallied, and conspired to chase him over a cliff. The body of the giant man had been fished from the sea. His death was recorded as accidental, a rat cornered with nowhere to run. I nodded at the events recounted by the farmhands, watching the red berry juice run down my arm.

A new story then emanated from our wind-up radio out in the fields. The police were searching for a local man who had gone missing somewhere on the coast. His wife was appealing for help and information. The missing person was quite famous, a photographer called Emil Gironde, someone I recalled from my studies. Search teams were combing the nearby area on foot and were expected on the farm soon. My friends kept me updated while we loaded baskets of fruit into trailers.

The next day, I was eager to leave. Tone had laid out breakfast on the kitchen table, but I stood ready to go at the door, dressed in the grey tracksuit and grey hooded top she had donated. I thanked her, in Norwegian, for helping me out, and voted my thanks to her husband and his crew again for saving me, mispronouncing the words from a note I had composed with much help. She smiled and looked a little teary as she packed my breakfast in a bag. We walked down the path from her house to the fjord, where we hugged goodbye. A bus took me to Tromsø.

In the city I trailed tourist groups around the cathedrals,

1

museums, and other landmarks, attracted by the sounds of the English-speaking guides. In the evenings, I practised what I had learnt in the day and listened closely to the guide's patter on the next tour. After a while, I knew as much about Tromsø as the guides. Gossip in the evening bars led me to Anders. He handed me an official guide badge and I started my first tour the next morning. The group were a mix of Europeans whizzing around the top ten attractions in the Paris of the North, as I learnt to introduce the city. Anders gave me a phone, and the key to a house where I, and other, illegal immigrants slept. He arranged further work as a guide. In return, I gave him half my earnings from the tourist centre, and nothing else, unlike other people tempted by more money.

I called the mother and father hotline, and a short time later, a replacement passport arrived in a brown padded envelope, delivered to the main Posten Norge in the city. The clerk accepted the ID presented on my phone; I was a legitimate person again. I grinned as I remembered trying to post the report on Alexander to my client in Cambridge. Those were the days when I was footloose and fancy free. To blow with the wind was my aim.

All was fine for a week, then the fits came back. The first was in public, in the nave of the Domkirka. Some thought I lay quivering out of religious fervour; others saw that I frothed at the mouth and bit my tongue. Anders was not pleased. He waited a couple of days before sending me back out to work. The next time I simply fainted, falling like a sack of potatoes in front of a group of tourists at the Polar Museum, who laughed hard, until they saw the dark, spreading stain on my trousers. Anders took away my badge, phone, and key, and I never saw him again. I was left with some cash stuffed inside my passport. That night, the lowest I have ever endured, I heard the name Sigrid again. There was no one else in the room.

When the fishing boat carrying me pulled into the little harbour, and drew up at the quay, I had a tremendous sense of *deja vu*. The day's light was the soft glow of a lightbox and the sea, sky, houses, and boats were all sharply defined. The water, although deep, was clear enough to see the bottom of the harbour. I was happy to step off the boat on to the solid wooden planks, and while I felt giddy for a moment, my balance returned soon enough. This side of the harbour was a single tall cream house, with large doors, some sort of factory. On the opposite side of the harbour was a long line of wooden houses, all built up on another wooded stilted quay. The houses were mostly white, otherwise the deep colour of orange, red and brown mud. A line of orange buoys bobbed in the harbour, beyond which there were two other boats in the harbour. These craft were sleek and gleaming white; they suggested tourists taking fun rides, not the hard work of fishing the sea.

Behind the row of houses, the grassy hills rose to an impressive height, and in the middle, somewhat on its own, sat a large white house. The old man who had brought me over from Tromsø in his boat called to me. 'Sigrid,' he said, and he hooked a thumb upwards.

'Takk.' There is always someone in charge, in any place you visit, and Sigrid was known for her charity to others. I walked around the harbour, looking out for English-speakers, but heard only local accents, and saw smiles of welcome. The houses around the quays and wharfs were in good shape, well maintained and painted. But as I walked up the path into the hills, I saw that the houses behind the facade of the picture-book harbour were run-down, squalid, disused. There was evidence of restoration work: scaffolding up to the rooves, lumber placed in neat piles, one side of a house freshly painted.

A middle-aged woman stepped out on the path in front of me. She was in her fifties, with thick auburn-amber hair that framed her head. 'Stop there, please,' she said, smiling like a pleasant policeman.

'Sure,' I said, 'I'm just visiting Sigrid.'

The woman shook her head. 'Not today. It's not a good day.'

I looked at her, examining a face tanned like supple leather. 'Are you Sigrid?'

She shook her head. 'I'm her sister, Siv. Sigrid is having the day off.'

'What does she do when she's working?'

Siv turned and waved her hand across the harbour. 'She rebuilds this place.'

'On her own?' I smiled my brightest smile.

'With the help of visitors. They build, they paint, they restore the buildings.'

'I can paint. I'm an artist.'

She looked at me for a long time. 'Ah, you're English. You reminded me of someone else.' She struggled to be happy, and welcoming, but there was something on her mind. She pointed down to a house the colour of ochre. 'There is food and water in the house. Heinz will show you. Tomorrow you can help us.'

'OK, thank you.' No questions were to be asked, I was welcomed as a traveller who needed a job. Perhaps this place would be as easy as picking fruit on Tone's farm.

Siv turned and started back up the hill.

I called out behind her: 'Tell Sigrid that I'm sorry for her loss.'

Siv stopped and turned around. 'How do you know about that? I suppose people have been talking.'

'Your bracelet, the colour of blood, in remembrance of someone who is lost.' I was guessing, but the air in this place had a tension about it, as did Siv. The red bracelet, made of wood or ivory, I could not tell which, could have been a party bangle for all I knew. But it happened that I hit the nail on the head.

'What is your name?'

Names, identities, characters. Chance, necessity. Which way was the wind blowing today? I raised the ante by asking my own question. 'What was the name of Sigrid's son?'

I've only ever seen this look, of awe, of realisation that the speaker is on another plane, on one other's woman's face before. The woman was Ruth, years ago in that wine bar, when I had an idea about her work that would help her out.

'Svein,' she said quietly.

'How did he die?'

She looked away over the sea. I had to move closer to hear her voice. 'He had health problems, from an early age, his heart.' She looked up at the white house.

I did not ask any more questions. Svein's death was not recent. Sigrid's sister had not been crying, the skin around her eyes was not puffy, and she could talk about Svein without faltering. The red bracelet was an anniversary totem.

Here, Sigrid engaged with the world through others, letting them do the work of young men. I was a welcome young man, who, tomorrow, would be painting one of the fishing huts down below. I suddenly felt deeply sorry for Sigrid, an emotion that surprised me, considering that I did not know her. But then, do we need to meet all the lonely people of the world to feel empathy towards them?

Siv pointed down to the harbour. 'Heinz is down there.' She turned and walked up the hill to the white house.

My stomach ached, and my mouth was dry. I wandered back down the hill, turning plans over in my mind for tomorrow. I was an itinerant worker in a disused Norwegian fishing village, accepted as a case of charity. I expected to meet other similar travellers, and I was not disappointed. Heinz was at the door to the ochre house; I did not even have to ask his name. He had a thick, bushy, walrus moustache, and was joined by another bald man of the same thick build. The image of leaping from the frying pan into the fire occurred to me. You wish to blow with the wind, Alexander, then you must live your life in line with the roll of the dice and see where that leads.

Heinz explained how the place worked. There were three meals a day, and a bed with a mattress in the large white house where I arrived. In return for the food and board, I would provide labour and follow Heinz's instructions. I was not to disturb the artists who visited, or get in the way of the holidaymakers, even though I fitted both categories. I was welcome for one month, then I should think about moving on. The island provided respite, for those who needed a break from their life.

I picked up a can of undercoat and got to work. There was bean soup for lunch, with mysterious green leaves floating in it. The bread they served was long-life, made by robots in factories. I resumed work, happy to play my part for a while.

This was not to be one month of painting and sawing and,

inevitably, avoiding Heinz's attention. Sigrid was the boss woman; always go for the boss and see what she wants. She had lost Svein, her son, a young man around my age. Had he been an artist, too? Or a labourer? Or someone else? I reflected on my wide-ranging interests in arts and psychology. There was now a need to break new ground, to shock, to do something worthwhile that had real impact. I had an audacious idea forming, one that would help Sigrid move on.

And then I, too, would move on, riding up on the next breath of wind to goodness knows where.

CHAPTER 2

A nna looked at the solitary soup bowl on the table. As usual it was dinner for one, and a bone for the dog. Evenings were chilly now on the summer farm, midway up a valley, northeast of Tromsø. Outside the window, the sky over the Kvænangen fjord was blue and darkening in the autumn On a clear evening of continuous daylight during the summer, she could look down the fjord and see the southern islands. Now, autumn was departing and winter was on its way. She ate her soup in silence. Gunnar, a Great Dane, lay on the floor uninterested in food.

After dinner, she rested in the living room in her favourite seat, the rocking chair, with its comfortable red cushion tied up with bows at the corners. Emil's work still hung on the walls, photographs of sunsets: rich, yellow disks slipping behind dark treelines on the blood orange sea at the coast. Anna dragged out several albums of photographs from under the sofa. She looked at a photograph of Emil, taken on the day he went missing. He had long hair and a full beard, was dressed in his walking gear: blue waterproof trousers, a dark green jacket with a hood. She set the photograph on the mantelpiece and lit a candle beside it.

Inspector Rohde had sent her many photographs over the last three years, of young and old men with long hair and beards. None were Emil. She was rather surprised, and then disappointed by how much the police attached to an appearance so easily disguised or changed.

She closed the album. 'These are all the photos we have, Gunnar.' The Great Dane lay on the floor by her feet, chest rising and falling. 'It's a shame we didn't take more of each other.'

She put another couple of pieces of coal on the open fire and added a log, which cracked and hissed, sending yellow flames up the chimney.

'Have a told you about Emil? About his asceticism, and his

7

love.' Anna took a sip from a tumbler full of brandy. 'He was a wonderful, fascinating man, and I was lucky to know him.'

She took an envelope off the table and turned it in her hand. 'This is his Will.' She looked at the thick cream envelope. 'I've never opened it.' She took a larger gulp of brandy and winced as the spirit burnt her throat and the roof of her mouth. 'I suppose it's time. He's been gone nearly three years. What do you say?'

Gunnar snuffled in his sleep; his legs jerked, and tail flapped.

'I agree. It is time.' She took the envelope and a knife they used as a letter opener. The light glinted off the thin blade. Carefully, she slid the blade under the sealed down flap and cut through the top of the envelope. She placed the knife on the table and took out a sheet of paper, in the same stationary as the envelope.

'Look at how grown up we were. Nice stationary. Lawyers properly notified in Tromsø.'

She sat back down in the rocking chair. 'They say that a Will is a measure of how well you know someone. Now that he is gone, perhaps Emil will reveal his true nature to me.'

She unfolded the piece of paper and began to read. She read from top to bottom, then put the piece of paper on the table. The evening sky was dark outside. She looked at her reflection in the window, lit by the candles in the room. There had been evenings when she had imagined Emil sitting on the sofa, reading a book, or watching the television. But Emil would disappear whenever she closed the curtains.

Tonight, she left the curtains open and refilled the tumbler with brandy.

She returned to the rocking chair, feeling the effects of the alcohol, and wanting more. 'Let me tell you about what I have just read.' There was brandy dribbling off her chin. She wiped her clothes and put the tumbler on the floor.

'You will need to milk the goats, Gunnar, at this rate.' She laughed, and then her laughter turned to tears. She waved Emil's Will in the air. 'Do you think I found clues in here, Gunnar? Do you think he listed an unknown woman, or love child, or secret organisation, to receive part of his estate?'

She got hold of herself and waited until she could breathe properly. 'No? Then what do you think I found?' Gunnar woke up at the noise she was making and turned his head towards her.

'I'll tell you what I found. Details of his funeral arrangements!' She read the paragraph out loud. 'He wanted a Sami funeral. He wanted to be buried in a forest, in a procession with the shaman beating his drum with a silver stick. The mourners were to follow in a line and ring his body in a circle, singing a traditional song.' She let the tears and pain come and go. Her stomach was burning from too much drink and too little food. 'The song is called a joik, it is a song of dedication. He wanted Nina and Solveig to carry baskets of white flowers, and to lay a flower at every step. All the mourners were to wear flower garlands. It is a beautiful idea from a beautiful man.'

She went into the bathroom and threw up in the toilet. For minutes, she knelt spitting and crying into the bowl. When she had cleaned up the mess, she came back to the living room, and closed the door. The flame of Emil's candle guttered but did not go out.

Her eyes were red in the mirror above the mantelpiece. She picked up Emil's photograph again and held it to her chest. 'I am not bereft of comfort. I have family and friends. I have Birgit, Nina and Solveig. Siegfried and Fridtjof can help me with the farm. They have been patient enough.'

She collapsed on to the sofa and disturbed an old book of Emil's. The book was a photography manual, dog-eared, the stitching in the spine coming away. She read the inside front cover where he had written his past addresses. 'I still have one of his old haunts to check, Gunnar. It's in Oslo, but such a long time ago, is there really any point searching there?' She let the book fall to the floor. The book tipped on to the glass tumbler, which broke into several large pieces. She sat up on the sofa and put her foot down on the largest piece of broken glass.

Her cries of anguish echoed around the valley.

CHAPTER 3

I woke up in the small hours of the morning, prompted by a spring in the lumpy mattress poking through the fabric. The room smelt of fresh paint. By the side of each bed was a very welcoming bowl of fruit on a wooden locker. The lockers were made here; Heinz was teaching me how. I honestly had expected company in the night and had been prepared to wake up in an instant. In the end, it was a sharp stab of pain and the snuffling and snoring of people around me. The room had six beds, all iron frames, set on a blue linoleum floor. To my left was a young white woman, and in the bed next to her, a young black man. To my right were two beds, both taken by older men, shorter than me, who fought in their sleep with their breathing. An older woman occupied the remaining bed. We all went to bed at different times, but in silence, coyly turning away as we stripped down to t-shirt and underwear for the night. In the case of the older woman, she wore a nightdress and a nightcap.

The young black man, Frank, was the friendliest. He had been rebuilding one of the houses on the wharf, cutting and sawing timber, making roof joists. I had started with him as a painter, slapping undercoat on freshly assembled door frames.

The eldest woman, Marilyn, was also a painter, but not of houses. She was a proper artist, she said: willowy body, flyaway hair, ditzy manner. She went on about the light incessantly and stood looking at scenes with her fingers held up to make a square frame.

Once awake, I could not go back to sleep. I got up, slowly, my vision sparking with flashes of light, and went to sit in the kitchen. Marilyn had told me more about Sigrid. A talented dancer and painter, she had been knocked flat by Svein's death, at such an early age, not as a child, which is horrific, but as a young man, the man she had always dreamed he would become. She never got over it, and her muse fled to goodness knows where. Marilyn's goal in life was to reunite Sigrid with her muse.

Sigrid, however, seemed resigned to her fate and her new role as bereaved mother, although previously she was a happy humanist, directing the life of the village. She had loved life, and cheerfully accepted death as part of the natural randomness of the universe. What was there to fear of her own oblivion? But the oblivion of her only child was another matter. Svein's body had been cold in the hospital by the time she had got to see him again.

Just like that - gone. Marilyn snapped her fingers. Then she showed me a photograph of Sigrid and Svein together. Sigrid looked like Siv, her sister. Svein had staring eyes, thick blonde stubble, and receding blonde hair. I closed my eyes and remembered the face. When I opened my eyes, I confirmed the image, and returned the photograph to Marilyn.

Frank came into the kitchen. He wore a blue t-shirt and the black boxers he slept in. Marilyn turned away. He shared pop-up waffles with us, hot from the toaster. I made instant coffee, and we made our usual joke about whether he liked it black or white. As it turned out he fancied white today, long-life UHT milk from the fridge. Marilyn coloured up and left the kitchen. We laughed like kids.

Back in the dorm, I put on my trousers, day shirt, and sweater. I told Frank I would see him later to paint the new house. The air was fresh outside in the harbour, everything made clean again by the wind off the sea. The white house dominated the hills. The idea forming in my head was audacious all right. I couldn't recall anyone ever having done anything like it before in the history of the universe. For the rest of the day, I painted, sawed, and learnt new skills. At lunch time, while everyone else was outside, I went to the store at the harbour edge, in vain search of what I needed, and came up trumps.

My idea was homeopathic, a cure provided by a little bit of what ails you. People would ask how I could do such a thing to a woman. It would be considered the height of bad taste. Truth be told, I didn't have many options; I had to do something. I had three weeks remaining of free living here, and then I needed to be on my way. But to where exactly? This place was a tolerant oasis in a not particularly tolerant society, as my wanders around Bodø had confirmed. The police of two countries were interested in me. I wanted to stay and work at being me in this country. The force of this realisation surprised me. The wind-born seed wanted to put down roots.

I worked on my plan in the middle of the night, waking up at three o'clock, tiptoeing to the shared bathroom. I followed the instructions to the letter and hoped for the best, as many have in the past. 'Everything, alright?' asked Frank when I stole back through the room, hood up like a thief. 'You were in there a long time.'

I gripped my belly. 'What is in that bean soup?'

He laughed and turned over to go back to sleep. 'You don't want to know.'

I drank coffee, wolfed down a waffle, and left the hostel. The morning air today was refreshing in the extreme, a mist on the water. I shivered outside in my hoody, pulled up over my head. Halfway up the hill to the white house, I stopped, closed my eyes, and checked what I was about to do. I would sit in the garden of the white house, with my face turned away, and Sigrid and Siv would look out of the windows and ask: who is that? And then the rest was up to fate. At worse, Heinz and his friends would be called to haul me away, beat me up and put me on the first boat out. Or the police would be called, and a psychiatrist, who would ask: why do such a thing to a grieving woman?

I walked up the path and passed the front door of the little white house. My footsteps were noiseless in the turf, or was it moss, in the garden. There was a seat, roughly carved from a tree trunk, and I sat down, back to the house, looking out over the cliff to the sea. I knew that, behind me, there were four windows downstairs and four upstairs. I didn't think Sigrid or Siv would be armed; they made a business of taking in strangers, but what I was going to do might come as a bit of a shock.

Further down the garden path, under an apple tree, I spotted a stone plinth. I turned my head to the left and read the dedication to Svein Jurgsson: a life of thirty years, forever

12

with us.

Never a truer word, I thought.

CHAPTER 4

The next day Anna got up with a throbbing head, and a sore foot, heavily bandaged. She was determined to work away her pain, so she made the summer farm tidy and comfortable, swept the pine floors, arranged the cream woollen rugs around the furniture. Fridtjof, her neighbour, would be calling on her later. A table was laid out for tea in the kitchen, with a jug of milk from the goats that morning, and a cake she had bought from the store at the water's edge. In the living room, the sofa was readied for where a man and a woman could sit together, amongst the cushions decorated with hearts and pitchforks. And everywhere in her home, long white candles stood in brass holders, waiting for the last of the autumn nights, and the arrival of winter.

She rocked in the chair slowly, listening for the crunch of Fridtjof's boots on the hillside track. Moving on, she thought, was difficult when every unexpected sound could be that of Emil returning. She fingered the necklace she wore - tears of red gold on a golden chain, an anniversary present she found by accident a week after Emil had gone, hidden in a camera case.

Anna still remembered him standing in the doorway, before he left for the coast: the hug they had shared, the texture of the hat she handed him, the last kiss on the lips. When Emil had not called a day later, she was not so surprised. The journey might have been difficult. He may have got in late, coming back on a night boat, and then having to wait until day to move across country. Perhaps he decided to stay over somewhere. He was a charming man and could easily fix himself a bed for the night. In his younger days, he had camped in a tent, although he said he was too old to sleep out now, but really, he was too sensible. She presumed if the sunset had proven to be so spectacular, then the sunrise might be equally as good.

In the winters, when the sun really did take its leave, then things had been bad for her, at first unspeakable. But there had been one unexpected positive: her figure had improved, helped by a tall frame and a lack of interest in food. She had inherited a natural beauty from her mother. In her youth, her blonde hair had flown behind her. Now her hair lay down and was best combed flat and tied at the back. The gentle smoothness of her cheek had become creased, but when she smiled, her skin smiled around her green eyes. Her lips were thinner, but her heart was stronger. Three years without Emil, or even knowing what happened to him, had produced many tears, but she had survived.

Footsteps approached, boots crunching on the stones, then a knock at the door. She slid back the bolt. Fridtjof entered and took off his cap.

'Hei,' he said, grinning cheerfully.

Gunnar plodded through to the kitchen to lick Fridtjof's hand and receive a dog biscuit. Then the large brown dog lay down in its basket and was soon asleep, chasing reindeer, paws flapping.

Anna and Fridtjof sat down at the kitchen table. She served him tea and cake.

'It is getting colder. Will you be moving to your sister's place for the winter?' he asked.

'Not this year. The school in Burfjord has taken me on to teach English and Maths. I am looking forward to the new challenge.'

Gunnar barked a wet cough and fell silent.

'He's still sick,' commented Fridtjof.

'The cancer has moved to the lungs.''How long has he?'

'Not long.'

Fridtjof brushed Gunnar's coat with his hand. 'I'm sorry. I could get you another dog.'

'I do not need another.'

Fridtjof looked around the farmhouse kitchen. 'Your father only used this place in the summer. It is not suitable for a winter stay.'

'Well I'm quite stubborn and willing to give it a try.'

'You are a lone wolf,' said Fridtjof.

'Maybe all Norwegians are.'

15

Fridtjof shook his head. 'We do not live in a well populated place, that is true, but we are not anti-social, and we respect the weather.' He softened his tone. 'I know it has been difficult without Emil.'

'I have Gunnar.'

Fridtjof looked at the sleeping dog. 'Not for ever.'

'He will be in my memory for ever. Siegfried will come by with the post and bring me bread and coffee.'

'What about robbers or bandits?' said Fridtjof. 'They will expect a summer farm to be deserted. Or will you be the last tough girl in the valley?'

'You know there is no trouble here. The farms are quiet all year round. Occasionally, a lost hiker comes by, and I put them on the right track. I like the silence, I milk the goats, make some cheese, it is what I want to do.'

Fridtjof rubbed his chin, ran a hand over his short-cropped hair, and tried again. 'It's October tomorrow. It will be cold soon. There was five metres of snow last year, in this very place. It took days to uncover the roads. And you are not getting any younger.'

His reminder that the colder months were coming annoyed her. Like many others she loved the summer, loved it for the tangible improvement it made in her mood. She was good humoured in those precious months when her skin glowed, and she was a young woman again. Thoughts of the dreary twilight, and the long dark days of winter, these things upset her, and broke the spell.

'This is my home, Fridtjof, for a large part of the year, and now maybe all year round. My father bequeathed the farm to me, and I want to keep it working, not for it to become forgotten.

Fridtjof put down his cup of tea. 'You are still waiting for Emil; everyone can see it.' Fridtjof was gentle while he spoke. 'All things come to pass. It has been three years, dearest Anna; it is time for you to let go and move on.'

She left the kitchen and returned to the rocking chair in the living room. Gunnar did not move as she walked by. While Fridtjof finished his tea and cake, she rocked back and forth and looked out of the window, and studied the photographs on the mantelpiece: two young girls, her nieces, with hair the colour of wheat, in white dresses with long sleeves and ruched collars, Nina in a black waistcoat, Solveig in the red, both with silver brooches on the lapels.

She got up out of the chair and picked up another photograph, an oval portrait of Emil and her on their wedding day. She kissed his image. You and I met nearly twenty-eight years ago. And then one day, you were taken away from me. Why didn't you leave your body behind as some evidence of what happened?

She studied one of his photographs. What was so special about the sunsets where Emil visited? Did other people go along too? She had sought out photography clubs to ask their members. People knew Emil; he was an established photojournalist. Well published in magazines, and widely exhibited, he was known for his fascination with the setting sun and old rural buildings. His club members said that they would keep an eye out for him.

Fridtjof knocked on the door of the living room and she invited him in. He sat down on the sofa. Anna rocked slowly in the chair. 'Alva and I will look forward to seeing more of you, if you decide to stay in the winter.'

She smiled. 'Thank you. I will also invite Birgit and her children out here. Nina will lay a place for Emil at the table. Solveig will say a prayer.'

'We all say prayers for Emil.' Fridtjof sighed. 'A memorial service would be appropriate.'

She stopped her gentle rocking. 'Everyone is keen for me to move on and close the chapter on Emil, but I want to know more. Some missing people return many years after the event. There are families and friends who wait a lifetime for someone special to return.'

Fridtjof's mouth was moving but he said nothing.

Anna resumed her rocking. 'In term-time, I will walk to the school in Burfjord. There will be marking to bring home in my rucksack. Gunnar will keep me company for as long as he can. On the weekend, I will make some improvements to this place.' 'They are lucky, these children.'

She got up, crossed to where Fridtjof was sitting, and

squeezed his hand. 'You have been kind to me, but I need to wait a little longer for Emil.'

Fridtjof stood up and put his coat and cap on. 'Let's have dinner next week,' he said brightly. 'Alva will cook.' He went through to the kitchen where he put on his boots, tied his bootlaces, and walked out the door.

She went into the kitchen to see how Gunnar was doing. The dog was sleeping in his basket. Let peace come and stay with him.

She returned to the rocking chair. The TV was showing a repeat of the voyage of the Hurtigruten ship moving slowly up the coast, all one hundred and thirty-four hours of it, in real time. Emil had loved it.

She dared one of the shadows in the room to challenge her, to turn into Emil's ghost, and to scare her. She reasoned that such a happening would be the first recorded instance of a real ghost, and she would become famous.

She whispered: 'It is you I wait for. When will you be home?'

CHAPTER 5

I waited, watching as the mist rose off the sea, warm in the clothes I wore. My head itched a little, but that was to be expected. I could easily be mistaken for a common or garden trespasser, but here, where people were given a second chance, I did not expect any punishment. The apples were small, I was hungry, so I plucked the largest from a tree, branch bowing and then springing back, dropping leaves. The fruit was hard, bitter, and tart. The acid stung my lips and set my teeth on edge for minutes afterwards.

I heard the drawing back of a curtain. There was the knock of fingers on a glass window, a door opening. I wiped my mouth, and stood in a relaxed pose, hands in front of me. Footsteps approached, crunching on a path, and then tramping over the grass, multiple sets. I tensed, bowed my head, and closed my eyes.

Two bare feet appeared in front of me beneath the hem of a blue and white nightdress, the toenails painted red. There was a gasp as Siv's breathing quickened. Then another pair of naked feet joined the first, toenails also red but chipped. Such a sucking in of air followed, as if a person drowning had broken the surface and was now, after years, allowed to breath. I imagined a hand fly up to her mouth, but I did not look at Sigrid directly.

'Take your hood down,' said Sigrid. 'Face the sea.' I did as I was told, and the two women stood on each side and looked at me. Sigrid was wearing a green gilet over her pyjamas. She took something from the pocket.

If it was to be a knife across the throat, then I would die here, exsanguinated under an apple tree. It would be a shame, the waste of such a talent, but there was a limit to what the universe could take.

Instead, I felt her gentle hands on my head, and heard the snip of scissors. Blonde hair fell on my shoulders and chest, cut from around my temples. I was to be given a receding

19

hairline.

When Sigrid was finished, she said: 'Wait here. We will bring food. Face the house when you eat.'

I was to be the ghost after all. I was to be Svein, about whom I knew very little.

I brushed the newly dyed hair off my face with my hands. My party trick had worked. Here I was, the model made up ready to convince Sigrid that her son was alive but also at rest.

Siv brought me a plate of bread, sausage, cheese, banana, and a hot drink made with some type of berry. This was looking much more promising than being pushed off a cliff. I listened to the surf below, crashing over the rocks, gulls squawking in the rising wind. This was my chance. Do well here, in the most audacious of auditions, and I might survive, even prosper. Otherwise, I was at the road's end, an intruder in this country, and in this woman's life.

How would Svein have eaten? Was he right or left-handed? Did he have pleasant or unpleasant table manners? I ate the food, which was very welcome, while gazing at the windows of the house like I owned the place. I aimed to be the best of Svein. Go on, I said, remember me! You have cut my hair in his style; you know what I am trying to do. I am trying to mend the rift between two worlds. Come and talk with me. I am Svein. I am not a hungry hobo with nowhere else to go.

Siv returned after an hour and took away my untouched plate. I remained posed on the seat, looking at a spot somewhere above the downstairs window in the room where now Sigrid paced about. My back was killing me, but I could not slouch. Svein was late twenties with straight blonde hair that would recede in middle age, no beard, blue eyes. He had a look that asked of the camera: 'What now?' I could only guess that Svein might have a sense of humour, and surely the way to Sigrid's heart was through humour.

I channelled Laurel and tossed the banana skin over my shoulder: the flapping yellow wrapper sailed over the cliff. Hardy rolled his eyes at me and I slipped off the seat onto the ground. Was that laughter I heard?

The seat was carved from one piece of wood, an oak; the

seat of a king watching from the cliff top over the world. A competent piece but without any obvious sign of experience or expertise. Legs apart, back bent, I attempted to the lift the seat, and fell slumped forward beaten by the task, head on the ground, bottom in the air.

The door in the house opened again. I turned around and saw Sigrid walking out on her own towards me. She was just like Siv but with shorter blonde hair and wearing glasses. She was dressed now in canvas trousers, boots, and her green gilet. 'Hello,' she said. 'What are you trying to do?'

I straightened my clothes, cleared my throat. 'I am trying to be kind, because we are all subject to chance, to necessity, and because the situation demands it.'

Sigrid's face changed as she caught the foreign accent. She shrank a little into her green gilet like a turtle hiding away from a threat. 'Do you want money?'

I shook my head. 'To be good for nothing is the only way. Kindness is its own reward.'

There was movement near the garden gate. Heinz, Frank, Marilyn and others had arrived. Heinz looked like he wanted to send me over the cliff after the banana skin. Marilyn looked shocked. Frank was shaking his head, trying not to laugh.

Sigrid waved them to stop where they were. 'You speak about kindness. Do you know Bjarne?'

I turned the name over in my mind. Images and tastes came back to me: stew, pipe-smoke, large hat, looming face. 'Yes, I met him.'

'What animals would he keep if he could find them?'

'He would keep bees.'

Sigrid relaxed. 'So, it is you.' She walked around me, as if I were a mannikin in a department store. 'Sit down and talk with me.' I did so and looked over at the sound of Marilyn crying. Frank and Heinz were applauding. 'Thank you for what you are trying to do. It is a remarkable kindness.'

I did not say a word and wondered about Svein's relationship with his mother.

'When you died, all I wanted to do was climb in the coffin next to you.' She closed her eyes, and I saw that the skin was damp from tears. 'Siv stopped me, of course.' She looked back at the house. 'She's a wonderful sister.'

I sat silently, eyes scanning her clothes, trying to pigeonhole her by class and profession, as we did back home, but she was different. Her skin was tanned form the sun and wind. She wore a necklace of small shells.

'Do you remember when you carved this seat?'

It was now or never, the moment when the illusion would be maintained and displayed without a glitch or shattered like a mirror. I thought it best to close my eyes when I spoke. Nothing gives away a person like his or her eyes. 'Yes, I remember,' I said, imitating the sound of Anders speaking English in Tromsø.

I let those two words and the faked accent resonate with her. There was no abreaction; she did not flinch, or get up, howling at this imposter in her garden, made up to look like her beloved son.

'Tell me more.'

'Svein fell like a tree,' I had decided, 'a strong man cut down in his prime, literally like a tree. His heart had been weak; there was nothing he could do.'

Sigrid shook her head. 'He was an addict,' she said. 'Strong drugs, cocaine, maybe heroin.' Her voice trailed away.

'Svein was searching,' I said, 'for himself, like many men do. The drugs let him get closer to a peace of mind that allowed him to find his true point of being.'

'Very good.' Sigrig was nodding. 'Svein always said that he wanted to see things clearly. He loved this cliff because it was a boundary between worlds. He wanted to jump off.' Sigrid spoke calmly.

'To fly, like Icarus, close to the sun, to see all of the world, and survive.' I gambled.

'Then you fell. That was your story.' I noticed a tear running down her cheek, and she had shrunk again.

Siv approached. 'Please come inside with us.'

They mothered me for a while, sat me on a sofa in front of an open fire burning eucalyptus logs. I searched the walls of the rooms for photographs and other mementos that would help me write Svein's story. Siv got up and left the room, and

Sigrid and I got used to one another. There were a few family portraits, combinations of Sigrid, a thick-set man who I took to be her husband, and the young Svein. There were pictures of Sigrid and Siv with an older Svein. And there were photographs of Sigrid when she was a dancer in a tutu or leotard, on stage, or at the barre, stretching like an elegant swan. The mantelpiece held ceramics, small and large pots, splashed with paint, like desserts dressed in chocolate and cream.

'I tried to be like my father, the little I knew of him,' I said, forcing myself to be bold. 'A strong man, a woodcutter, afraid of nothing. A bear of a mine.'

'You were just like him,' smiled Sigrid. 'Your father was a big, powerful man, who didn't look after himself, and hid in the woods for days at a time.' Her voice was clear. The threads of Svein's life were being wound about me.

Siv called and Sigrid left the room to find her. I refused to look up to check how well I was doing. The fire had warmed me, and I was feeling drowsy and wary of a fit. These moments of nodding off sometimes escalated into thrashing on the floor. I stood up and walked about. There was no time for illness; Svein was alive again, for however long it took Sigrid to move on.

The morning mist had cleared from the cliff top. What would Svein have thought of the view? Had he literally wanted to go over the edge? I walked back out into the garden and stood on the cliff edge. To tremble on the edge of the abyss has been a fantasy of many people, to tempt oblivion. Svein had been tempted; I was not.

I returned to the solidity of the carved seat, too slight to play the part of a woodcutter's son for long. The crowd at the gate had gone, but Sigrid was watching from the house. She came out and sat next to me.

'I'd only just begun,' I said, slapping the seat. 'My plan was to work in wood, to make artefacts that showed the strength and dependability of trees.' Down below in the harbour the newly renovated wooden houses shone with fresh paint. 'It bothered you that I didn't join in with the housing project.'

'I didn't like it at all. My son should have been the foreman.'

'So, I spent time away, like my father, in the woods and forests, sourcing the wood for projects at home.'

'Then it all went wrong for you. You lost control. The rest is a well-worn tale.'

'Maybe I wanted to be like Jack, climbing the beanstalk, looking for new worlds, castles in the clouds.' I slapped the carved seat with my foot. 'But I made this unlovely seat instead. This was my level.'

Before I could react, Sigrid put her arms around me. The contact was surprising; I stayed still, and she pulled me towards her, resting her head on my shoulder. 'Yes, that was Svein.'

CHAPTER 6

When Anna opened the door, the chill of the evening air swept into the kitchen from the hillside. Gunnar stood unsteadily and Anna stroked his head. 'It's you and me again, boy.'

They walked up the track to the top of the valley above the farm. The wet air wrapped around her like a damp towel. She looked down at the farmhouse, a basic building that Fridtjof, and to some extent Emil, complained about. The buildings were primitive, that was true: plain wooden planks for walls, built up on thick stone slabs to keep the rats and other animals away. A single pipe vented the kitchen stove through the corrugated iron roof of the farmhouse. Shining in the mist; it was more like a barn: poorly insulated, draughty, and frozen in the winter, but it was hers, and she would keep it.

There was a wooden sign on the side of the farmhouse by the door, next to the red metal post box emblazoned with a golden post horn. *Nordstrom*: the white letters were painted on black, with the elevation of the place painted underneath: five hundred metres. Her father had been a trekker, obsessed with altitude: halfway between the giants who lived in the mountains, he liked to say, and the trolls who lived under the bridges over the fjords.

She continued up the hill, through the woods, pausing often for Gunnar to follow. Sheep skipped away as she approached, bells clanging and ringing around their necks. Once upon a time Gunnar would have given chase, but now he panted to keep up with her, and he was not interested in the smell of those thick creamy coats. Near the top, as he was failing, Anna reached down and guided him forward. He was half-dead already, mists closing around his life just as the mists hid the summit from their path.

At the top of the hill, where stones were piled high in a cairn, they stopped to enjoy a rest and the view. Here, children and adults alike had scratched their names in the sign-post for posterity: the largest scribble being from Robert and Andrea, neighbours of hers. She and Emil had left a small, bold heart with an arrow through it. Singletons too had made their mark: Bert, Lilly, Dirk.

Emil had liked this place, too. They would sit together and gaze over the fjord below and the sky above. A band of moist air blew over, and her face and hair were wet again from the mist. Gunnar perked up, nose in the air, sniffing scents, but he did not run. Together they looked out into the grey cur-tain, resting with their backs to the cairn. She hugged Gun-nar's head to her cheek as if he were a baby.

Lost on the coast, unable to find his bearings, trapped by the tide, washed out to sea, presumably drowned; this is what she had imagined for Emil. No body had been found, no clothes, nor the camera or rucksack he carried, so the chances of survival were deduced to be remote. Therefore, in response, she had stubbornly concluded it was possible, somehow, that he was alive. Anna reckoned she would have known if Emil had died: it would have been by instinct, the connection she had with him would have been broken. What was lacking in those early days was some momentous feel-ing, some cymbal crash, or gut-wrench, that signalled he had gone. Because she had not felt such a rupture, she happily told people Emil was still alive, just missing. Emil was not the type of person to just slip away. He was persistent in every-thing he did, she joked.

Three years later, the pain had diminished, even forgotten for days at a stretch. The connection was still there, but vague, undefinable, pulled thin, if not broken. Yet still there were times when she would startle at a movement in the shadows, or a sound at the door, and turn her head, ready for him to reappear.

She threw a stone into the mist. 'Ridiculous!' she shouted.

On the way down, the clouds blew away and she saw the fjord stretch out in the distance, with views of Burfjord and ice-capped Jokelfjord in the distance. As they walked, the rain started to fall, turning to sleet, making the hardened roots of trees slippery, and either side of the path oozed puddles of mud. So much water gushing down: from many waterfalls, cascading over rocks, seeping through dams made by unseen beavers, flowing under bridges made by the farmers. The cold was persistent and crept into her coat and boots. At one point during her descent, Gunnar slipped and stayed still, eyes closed. She helped him up and wished she was stronger so that she could carry the huge dog home. Gunnar looked at her with sad, rheumy eyes. 'Don't go,' she said, 'let me get you comfortable first.'

Back at the farm, Gunnar rested in his basket in the kitchen covered with his red blanket. He did not look up when she pushed the bowls of food and water near his nose.

Outside, the rain turned to sleet. She found enough dry spruce logs at the bottom of the woodpile under the lean-to and brought them inside. The firewood lit well enough in the tiled stove in the kitchen, and she helped the blaze along with small sticks and pages of the *Folkebladet*, the regional newspaper. The stove began to draw air and the fire increased. She rested on the floor, caressing Gunnar's head, staying with him as the evening darkened, and the sun slipped behind the horizon.

Gunnar did not want to eat. She raised a cup to his mouth and the water dribbled down his chin. After her supper, a potato and leek soup that was almost the last of her food, she got ready for bed. Gunnar walked with her to the bedroom and climbed one last time into her bed. She wrapped him in a blanket, and he went to sleep.

In the early hours, after a short night when she only half-slept, she woke up and looked outside. The sky was lit with a continual glow. She looked at Gunnar's body and listened for his breathing. She did this often throughout the night, catnapping for an hour or so each time, or sitting on the bed, or pacing the room. Then at one check, her head poised over Gunnar's head, she heard nothing, and she froze. Gunnar's chest was warm but still. She recoiled from the body and stood in the bedroom doorway.

Gunnar lay stretched out in the faint morning light. She swallowed her courage and walked to the bed, reached out and closed his eyes. He looked peaceful but now she noticed a smell coiling up into her nostrils: of damp fur, of intestinal gas, of hot and sticky blood, and she saw the stain on his muzzle, and the darkened sheets.

She retreated to the living room, where she shivered, rocking in her chair, tears falling from her face. She heard the silence echoing around the farm. She was the lost child, naked in the cold, terrified, abandoned, shouting at the walls. 'On my own, again!' she hurled at the implacable sky, at Emil's photographs. Fists grabbed her hair; nails scratched her scalp. She kicked the rugs and slapped the furniture with her hands. Her head was hot, her eyes blinded by tears. 'There is nothing for me!' she shouted. She held herself, arms wrapped around her body. 'Must everyone go,' she wailed.

When she was exhausted and quiet, she got up and took out the bottle of brandy. She poured a slug into another cut-glass tumbler. Then she took Gunnar's blanket from his basket, wrapped it around herself, and lay down on a woollen rug in the kitchen. The night wore on as the brandy burnt her throat. The bottle got lighter. She listened out for Gunnar's scratching and snuffling, but she knew from waiting for Emil that she waited in vain. Eventually she became too tired to move, and lay with her face on the floor, curled up like a child, watching her breath evaporate on the tiles.

CHAPTER 7

Sigrid was at my side when I awoke, a cup of steaming berry juice in her hand. I sat up and took the cup. The drink was sweet and restorative.

'Svein hated berry juice.'

'People's tastes change,' I said, putting the cup down on the floor. The fire was embers only, day dull outside.

'People change their tastes to help others,' she said. 'Thank you.' She left the room and was replaced by Siv.

'You have done a remarkable thing, man who is not Svein' she said. 'I have never heard of anything like it.'

I rubbed my face and touched my hair. I didn't want to look in a mirror, because I would see Svein who would soon die of a heart attack.

'You cannot stay here any longer.' Siv said the words pleasantly. 'We are getting closed down. Too many illegal immigrants.'

I felt tired again, the long road ahead of me. I sat up, remembering that tiredness was a warning and a trigger.

'We have a friend who you can stay with.'

'More charity?' I asked. 'I need to make my own way.'

'He would like someone to record life in his villa.'

Siv was dressed in a blue suit with a yellow blouse. She looked professional, the mediator of Sigrid's strange therapy session.

'Will Sigrid be OK?' I asked.

Siv nodded. 'She's talking openly about Svein now.' She waved at the walls of the room. 'Soon more of his photographs will re-appear.' I could feel her eyes bearing into me. 'You have a big heart, big enough for the whole world.'

I went to the bathroom. The man in the mirror laughed at me. Hello, blondie! Nice haircut, shame about the roots. It was a new me, with a new beginning. But where was I going?

Siv called me to lunch, and we sat outside, behind the house, on a large table carved from oak, and on similar seats to the one near the cliff. We had filmed our scenes together. Post-production beckoned.

'Heinz will take you to a bus stop on the E6 near Rotsund. You will meet a man called Martin at noon. Here is his number if you need it.'

'The owner of the villa?'

'No, his assistant. The owner's name is Berkeley.'

'Everyone needs an assistant,' I said, finishing my meal.

Sigrid and I hugged. The bristles of my blonde beard scratched her face. She turned away without a word and went back to the house. I shook hands with Siv, like two professionals complementing one another on a job well done. Like I made a business of hiring myself out as a cure for death.

'Good luck,' she said, and gave me a leather pouch with one thousand krone inside. 'Make something of yourself. You have all the skills.'

I have too many skills, I am a dangerous man. I could do anything.

Heinz was waiting at the quay. 'So, you're leaving. That is a shame.' He looked me up and down.

'You'll find someone else,' I said, but he didn't hear me. After a short boat trip, Heinz pointed the way along the E6 to the bus stop, a yellow pole on the side of the road. 'Martin will meet you there,' he checked his watch, 'in an hour.' He gave me a curt wave as he returned to Sigrid.

The bus stop had no timetable, only a black 24 on a white sign on top of the pole. A few cars rolled by, and I looked out for someone who might be stopping early and who might be called Martin. Even if Morten turned up again, he would never recognise me. I was disguised by my new Scandinavian look. I really did have the chance of a new beginning.

The bus stop was on the corner of the road, and the sea broke over the rocks below me to my left. I clambered down the slope and was out on the rocks and the slow slope into the surf. This place was paradise. Blue sky, gleaming sands, granite rocks. I couldn't believe my luck! I had been invited to work with someone here in my new country. That would take care of any legal issues. I was welcome here; someone wanted me for my skills! I had money in my pocket, and a new passport. I was legal. I had finally found my way in the world, although I will admit the route was a little random.

I spotted something floating in the water. The object bobbed up and down and was finally washed up on the surf and sat on the sand, half in and half out of the water. I walked across the rocks, and then the wet sand, to find out what it was. The object was tossed towards me on the tips of the waves. It was a mass of fibrous material that sank down on the beach like a ball of wire wool. Unrolled, it turned out to be a large black coat with arms and a hole for the head.

I moved away from the shaggy coat, shrinking back to the rocks, waiting for the waves to deliver its owner: bloated, bitten by sea creatures, gasping for air, reaching out to the world, trying to hold on. Nothing more emerged from the sea. The mountain man had been filled with the freezing water of the Arctic sea and been pronounced dead on a trawler out at sea. The moment needed no commemoration. I scrambled away from the totem as if it had the power to take my own life.

There was a man waiting by a car when I got back to the road. He introduced himself to me as Martin. He was a short happy looking fellow, with tufts of white hair sticking out from around his ears and bald head that made him look like Schopenhauer.

'Are you Alexander?' he asked.

What a question! Once upon a time, yes, but life moves on. 'Call me Sacha.' I extended my hand, and he gave it a warm, welcoming shake.

'You come highly recommended from Sigrid. I hope we will be able to find you something fitting of your talents.'

I nodded and did not further comment. The car was warm. Martin was clearly benevolent. I was on my way.

CHAPTER 8

It was midday when Anna finished burying Gunnar. She returned inside the farmhouse to wash the soil from her hands. She shuffled around the place, as kettles boiled on the wood stove in the kitchen, and were emptied, refilled, and boiled again as she waited for the bath to fill. The radio in the bedroom provided some solace, a classical station to soothe her.

No-one believed that dogs went to heaven or enjoyed an after-life. Gunnar's bones would be a hidden testament under the stones.

A pain gripped her foot. The wound from the smashed glass tumbler went deep. Serves me right, she thought, as she changed the dressing. She was bothered by Gunnar's death. His body was lifeless, already changing into something else, but she imagined a misty dog rising from the ground, coming back to haunt her.

Suddenly, she stood up, and pressed down on the bandaged foot. 'I have had enough of death,' she announced to the walls. 'I want to be strong. I do not want to fear the dark or dead bodies.'

She locked the doors, bolted the windows, and got into the bath, her bandaged foot hanging off the side. She didn't imagine she looked very seductive.

The radio was on the classical station again. Valkyries removed Gunnar's humiliated body from the battlefield. The prelude to the first act of Lohengrin sweetened the air and injected life into her limp body. Violins pulled at her heart strings, took centre stage, and calmed her down. Gunnar was gone, even though she could smell him in the house. How many evenings had they spent, grieving woman, and dying dog, sharing Anna's taste in music, or her reading a book, or watching the television; how many walks had they enjoyed before bed? She was sure Gunnar had enjoyed a happy life; his energy when rounding up the sheep or chasing grouse was proof of his contentment.

The music from Lohengrin swelled, and with it, her tears flowed. Her wailing was drowned out by the surging tidal wave from the orchestra. She hid her face under a wet flannel until the music subsided and the bath water was cold.

What to do next would occur to her when the time was right. There was a list of possibilities in her head: call Birgit and talk about the future, call her colleagues at the school and talk about work. She could even agree with Fridtjof and arrange a memorial service for both Emil and Gunnar.

There were two finger taps on the windowpane in the kitchen.

Emil?

Could it really be?

No, it was impossible. Emil was gone. Beside there was another more likely explanation. Siegfried was due with the post at midday. She had locked the door to the kitchen, so he had tapped on the window. She clambered out of the bath, threw a towel around her, and walked into the kitchen.

Siegfried was indeed standing outside the kitchen window, the rain running off his peaked cap and dark cape. She let the elderly postman in and took the letters from him.

His dark eyes rested on her tear-sodden face. He looked at the two empty metal bowls washed up on the kitchen drainer. 'He's gone?'

She nodded.

He came over and kissed her on the forehead.

'Thirteen years, a good life.'

She closed her eyes and tensed, waiting for the next question about Gunnar.

'Anything you want, just give me a call,' he said. 'Have you got enough food in the house?'

There had been times when she had survived on next to nothing. 'I've got soup and bread. And brandy.'

They laughed and she hugged Siegfried to her, not wanting to let him go. A pulse of his warmth and his smell reminded her of Emil.

'You'll be all right,' he said. His eyes shone bright, this friend who had watched her grow up, get married, lose her husband, and now again today another loss. 'You're the toughest girl in the valley.'

'I don't want to be tough,' but she did not carry on, because she would have said, 'I want to be loved.'

Siegfried spread the newspaper out on the table. 'The weather doesn't look so good. Snow is expected soon on the high ground.'

'You'll need your skis and your sledge soon.'

Siegfried nodded. 'And the plough.'

'I thought Petter was driving the plough?'

'He hurt his leg. It will be up to me.'

'Why not ask one of his sons to help, like Steinar?'

'It's no trouble.'

Anna smiled. Siegfried could claim more from the government for two community jobs, which was a better deal than working as a farmhand. He sat down, and she placed a cup of black tea and a jug of milk next to him.

He noticed the half-finished roll of toilet paper on the table. 'I'll bring in some proper tissues for you tomorrow.' He drank his tea, and they caught up on news about the farms in the area. Then he got up, gave her another hug, and left. Moments later she heard his footsteps crunch away down the track. Emil, Gunnar, Fridtjof and Siegfried, all leaving the most fragile girl in the valley. The tears began to flow again.

By evening, after changing station and listening to some jazz on the radio, she finally had the stirrings of an appetite. In the kitchen she found a can of tomato soup and a loaf of bread. It was a proper loaf from the baker near the church down at the water's edge, but it had gone dry save for a spongy bit in the middle. She broke the bread in two and tore out the best piece. She warmed up the soup and ate it with a spoon from the pan, with what was edible of the bread. Her appetite expanded, surprising her; she finished the whole can.

She had another look at the photography book. A long trip to Oslo. One final address to check. He was a student when he lived there, but surely her trip would be pointless? How can I find out anything about Emil when the police have failed? We searched for weeks after his disappearance. No clues were found. I am a soft middle-aged teacher. When I am not teaching, I milk goats and make cheese. What can I add to the equation? The glacier is vast, and I don't even know where Emil was headed. I never questioned him. I had no reason not to trust him.

She got up early the next morning and milked the goats. Silje and her flock were put out to graze in the orchard. The milk was stored for later. Then she put on her coat and boots, and walked around the head of the valley, to where Tuva, Steinar's wife, gave her a lift in her car to Burfjord. From there she took the train to Tromsø and on to Oslo.

With each approaching high-rise building, she confirmed why she lived in the country. From Central Station in the Norwegian capital, she took the T-banen to a neighbourhood where Emil had lived a long time ago. She had found the address written in the inside cover of one of his photography books, a memento he had made during his way through life. The subway was half-busy, and she was half-convinced that the trip was a bad idea. But Inspector Rohde had asked her to leave no stone unturned. That meant she was to follow up all leads, all clues, and hunches.

She got off the subway, found the main street, took a left, carried on until the second right and walked down the road whose name was on her piece of paper. It was a tidy street with an electric car outside each small house. She tripped over a charging cable as she tried to dodge around a tree. The subway line ran across the bottom of the road. Emil's old house must have been noisy. This was such a far cry from the summer farm where the air was pure, and the sheep and goats made the only sounds.

I'm chasing a ghost, she thought. Emil is most likely dead, yet I cannot let him go.

There was a woman sweeping the street at the end of the road. She looked up at Anna and then resumed her work.

'Hei. I'm looking for someone. Can you help me?'

She showed the woman the photo of Emil. The woman studied his face: solemn eyes, beard, long waves of brown hair falling on to his shoulders. She shook her head. 'What's his name?'

'Emil Gironde. He lived here a long time ago.'

'I've not seen him. He is handsome though.' She flashed a toothy smile.

Anna thanked the woman who picked up her broom and resumed sweeping.

Emil's house appeared to be lived in, so someone might know something. She knocked on the door. There was no response. The woman had stopped sweeping. 'I think a lot of students live there,' she said. Small rooms, not much of a garden.'

Anna nodded. 'Of, course. Thank you.' She took one more look at Emil's old house and walked back up the road. She retraced her path to the subway, and thought about what she would do, if, miracle of miracles, she did happen to find Emil. Unless he had been abducted or imprisoned against his will, or slightly more likely, had suffered some medical accident that robbed him of his senses, then he had some explaining to do. Where had he been for the past three years? Why hadn't he got in touch? She stopped and steadied herself with a hand on a low wall. She was a fool. Emil was dead. Either that or he had abandoned her for some unfathomable reason and was living a new life. She didn't really believe either scenario, certainly not the latter. Someone had done this to him. Someone had abducted or killed Emil. But why?

On the train back to the city centre, a young couple sat in front of her. The woman caressed the back of the man's head as he played a game on his phone. Would she caress Emil's head if he returned? The young woman caught her eye and they smiled at one another.

Yes, she would welcome him back. She would forgive him anything. Someone had taken him away from her; it was not his fault. The logic of her abduction argument strengthened and placed the responsibility of his disappearance on an unknown assailant. Perhaps there had been a mugger, an opportunist, on the ice, who had taken an interest in Emil hiking on the glacier. An unfortunate or unspeakable accident ensued. Doleful Inspector Rohde had assured her that the strangest, most awful things happen, to the best people.

The train ran on and the likelihood of her scenario fell

apart. He had kissed her goodbye on that day for the last time. He was hiking across the glacier to photograph a collection of abandoned buildings on the coast. That was his thing. The silent building. The house that said to you whatever you said inside. She liked his idea, his unique selling point, and others did too. People gave meaning to situations, to images, to suit themselves.

She supposed there was a finite chance of meeting a homicidal psychopath in a barely inhabited national park but in practical terms such an event seemed impossible. There was more chance he had been taken by wolves or gored by a rutting reindeer. But still those odds were small enough to be zero. Emil was used to the country. He had a good sense of direction and was physically fit. While there was always a chance of many types of cardiovascular disease, cancer, and respiratory infections, he was no more likely to die than her.

So, that left death by misadventure, suicide, accidental fall, drowning, poisoning, fire, or alcohol.

She had Inspector Rohde's list of causes of death folded in her jacket pocket. She ran through each one. Emil rarely drank. It is difficult to make a life-threatening fire on a glacier. Accidental poisoning was unlikely as there were no toxic plants or animals en route. Emil was not on any medication. Drowning was possible, though, as he was visiting the coast. More bizarre accidents could happen, of course; like slipping and falling on the point of an ice axe, but the chance was slight. Suicide she ruled out; he had no reason to kill himself. He had gone missing three days before their twenty-fifth anniversary. She had turned over in her head every aspect of their relationship, and of his life, and had concluded that Emil was happy. That left death by misadventure and, reluctantly, she moved the chance of drowning to number one spot.

When she got home in the evening, she drew up a bucket of water from the well. Straight from the fjord, the cool liquid was crystal clear and clean to drink. Above the hills, behind the crest and the mountains on either side, was the great glacier. A vast place, which Emil liked to traverse on his trips to the coast to find interesting buildings or other features to photograph. She splashed some water on her face and down her neck.

I'm chasing a ghost, she repeated. Emil is dead and I cannot let him go. That is my mantra.

She called Birgit. 'I have been to Oslo today. The last address in Emil's book. I finally went.'

'And?'

'A dead end, no-one in. Emil never invited me to that house; he said it was too small. It's all bed-sits for students, with a subway nearby. A waste of time.'

Her sister was patient with her. 'Not a waste of time. You've ticked that list now.'

She drank the cool water and looked out of the window. The glacier shone illuminated by both the sun and the moon.

There was a pause between them. She waited for her sister to ask what she would do now, but Birgit was tactful. Instead she told Anna about how the glacier above the summer farm was melting.

'It has been melting for years.'

'The ice is giving up its secrets, Anna. From Kaevenengen to Oksfjord, and all around, the glacier is shrinking, leaving bare rock where once was blue ice. Pottery, arrowheads, clothes, old leather shoes, these are all being found.'

'We have had the same. Emil once found an arrowhead from the Viking past.' She picked up the metal object on the kitchen windowsill. 'I've even heard of a funeral for a vanished glacier in the south, a requiem for the missing ice.'

'That is not all that is being found, Anna.' Birgit paused. 'The bodies of people from long ago are being released from the ice.'

Anna poured herself a full tumbler of brandy. The vapour went up her nose and made her cough. 'Whereabouts?'

'Everywhere the glacier has been. The ice has held many secrets over the centuries.'

She took a slug of brandy and welcomed the burning liquid like an old friend. Outside there were the noises of farm animals and their predators. She admired the amber liquid in her glass: dutch courage they called it, to go into battle, ask a girl out, do something brave. For what did tomorrow bring for Anna? There could be no more moping about on the farm, flinching at every strange noise, banging her head against the inevitability of death. Emil, her friend and husband had gone, vanished. Gunnar, her companion and grieving partner, had gone, deceased. There was nothing anyone could say or do to make the situation any better. She felt for the connection with Emil and this time it vibrated, like a rope bridge across a gorge.

The goats would need to be moved down to another farm where Fritdjof would look after them. She would leave her summer farm open; Siegfried could look after it.

Another slug of brandy and her mind was made up.

'Gunnar's dead.'

'Then go.'

CHAPTER 9

It was a good time to leave, Anna told herself, as she dressed and packed her rucksack. When she had her boots on, and her skis and walking stick were ready, she stood outside the farm on the hillside track and looked over the fjord. The sparkling blue water stretched out to the horizon and the larger body of the Kvænangen fjord. Above the fjord, the summits of ice-topped Jokelfjord were visible through whispers of cloud. She stood ready in her brown Merino wool jumper and black leggings.

Even if she really had no chance of finding out what had happened to Emil, at least the goats were pleased to see her. They skipped about as soon as she opened their pens. She kept hold of Silje, the eldest, and tied her to a post in the shed, while she filled up the plastic feeder with grain from the feed bin, scooping up enough dry brown pellets until it was three-quarters full. The feeder was attached, and a clean milk pail found. The other goats, Sniff, Snork, Snuffkin and Tove, were now out in the orchard, under the plum tree. She caught hold of Silje's collar and led her to the milking stand. Silje knew the routine: she poked her head through the hole in the milking stand where she could eat out of the feeder. Anna wiped down the goat's udders with a wet cloth soaked in a clean bucket of boiled water, removing little scraps of straw and manure. The goat stood still and continued eating as Anna gripped the two teats and sent the first stream of milk onto the floor. Then the milk let down in earnest and sprang into the pail with a metallic ring. When she was finished, and the goat's udders were flaccid, she picked up the pail and put it safely out of the way.

'Good girl,' she said as she let Silje out of the milking stand and led her back to the orchard, with a scratch under her chin.

When she had milked the other goats, and finished with three full pails, she called Siegfried on her mobile.

He sounded surprised when he answered. 'Yes, Anna.'

'Hei. I'd like a favour, please.'

'Anything for you.' Siegfried had always been kind. She had always admired his rustic ways: how he whittled wood, how he talked to the animals, how he treated his wife like Queen Sonja, with boat rides on the fjord, and drinks and dinners.

'I'm going away for a while. I need someone to take care of Silje and her flock. Can you do that?'

'Of course. When are you going?' Siegfried sounded serious, almost worried.

'Very soon. I've done the morning milking. There are three buckets in the cool shed.'

'You're going now?' He stopped short of saying anything to stop her going. 'Of course, we will look after the place for you.'

'You can make brunost with the milk, or whatever you like.'

She ended the call and went back inside the farmhouse for the last time. The sky had brightened little since her early start. It was the wrong time of year to search for anyone, with winter coming, but action was the key, she concluded, to her predicament, wherever her adventure might lead her. She laced up her walking boots, took up her rucksack, walking stick and skis, and headed out. Siegfried would not arrive for a few minutes. She looked around the farm, saw how it was a dream showing its age. The wooden boards that made up the walls were stained with moss. The old corrugated iron roof was warped and bent, and in the winter conducted away any heat out of the building. She should sell the place to Fridtjof and be done with it.

Birgit and her girls would welcome her in; they all got on well together. But that possibility was for the future. Whatever the outcome, as her cut foot reminded her in its insulated boot, she had to move forward and not go back. She said goodbye to the summer farm, to the candle she had placed in the window and lit every year on the anniversary of Emil's disappearance, and strode upwards.

She had not gone far up the hill when there was a voice in the distance, and she stepped behind a tree to hide. There was the crunch of boots on the track. It was probably Siegfried coming up to take care of the goats at once. But when she looked down and peeped out from behind the tree, she saw Fridtjof walking up the slope in his slow way, hands on his bad knees. For a man of sixty he was very fit, loved his walking, and was dressed in a red checked shirt with an old brown jumper tied around his waist. He had on his dark grey working trousers and farm boots. She saw that he carried an envelope, in which she knew there would be a formal invite to dinner. She groaned, not that she disliked him or his family; Alva was a good woman, and a great cook, a skill she envied, but today she wanted to go, to disappear away from it all.

'Anna?' called Fridtjof, the long vowels of her name hunting for her in the house, the shed, the outbuildings. She stood still, like a little girl, guilty of what she had done with Gunnar, and cross because Fridtjof would not understand.

Silently, she picked up her rucksack, spread the rain cover over it, adjusted how she carried her skis, and resumed her climb up the hill away from the summer farm, melting into the bushes and away from her zealous neighbour. When she was a long way up, she poked her head through the branches of a tree and looked out. Fridtjof was knocking on the door. When he found it unlocked, he went in. A couple of minutes later he came out, and stood in that way of his, looking puzzled. He was such a good man, she felt awful about running and hiding away. More than ever she knew how the children felt when she had to tell them off, or even scold them.

She could see that Fridtjof did not hold the envelope anymore; it would be left on the kitchen table propped up against the empty flower vase. He would have looked around the clean kitchen and have begun to wonder. She had left a little subterfuge: the card of the therapist by the phone on the kitchen table and a street map of Tromsø open. Dr Gudjohannson, bereavement counsellor; Fridtjof had once implored her to attend. So, she left him thinking she had taken his advice and gone to see the shrink.

Perhaps he would believe her clues, perhaps he would be taken in. Their little falling out yesterday would be forgotten, and in return an invitation to dinner would smooth things over, and afterwards maybe a trip out across the fjord with Siegfried in his boat. Fridtjof looked all around, nodding his head, as if he understood, and then she saw him walk down the hill, with knees bent out and crooked legs turned in, the way the Sami walked downhill to soften the strain.

CHAPTER 10

A h, my Hasselblad. Lovely name. Great camera. Took a great shot of Anna in her swimming costume on the beach. Turned to jelly. Fell in love.

The two buildings I had visited near the coast on my latest trip, remnants of a farm once there, had interested me for a while. I looked forward to telling Anna all about it. With the naked eye, they appeared to be merely a house and a barn set close together. When the shots were taken, and the infrared film developed, the two buildings would appear as only one structure. The front of the house would be completely black with three jagged peaks to the roof. The corrugated roof of the barn, with its stripes vertical to the viewer, would be in shades of lighter grey. I saw sharks breaching the surface of the sea. I wondered what other viewers would see, and that was the point of a photograph by Emil Gironde.

Isolated buildings dominated my work. My photograph of the half-ruined house was a favourite. Red bricks built up in thirty neat rows perfectly tied together with white mortar. The wooden roof made of twenty planks of various lengths. A complicated chimney with a large round hat and a pyramid on top of it inspired some to think it Russian, others Chinese. Once the process of interaction started, it became the viewer's chimney.

Half of the wooden roof is shattered, planks skewed across the neat patterns. A once proud building has suffered damage. Did something crash into it? Has it been neglected? An idea flashes across the mind: No Place Like Home? It is now the viewer's photograph.

Another favourite photograph: the treehouse shot through a fisheye lens, the entire structure captured and wrapped up inside a sphere. The reflection of the flashlight beaming back out from the treehouse centre, frustrating and then adding to the photographer's attempts to capture the image. Idyllic childhood? Long summer evenings? Psychedelic music? Or the feeling of vertigo? Imprint on it what you will.

The simplicity of the image. The eye is drawn to one thing only, and for a while, it is the only thing of interest. Your personality makes it interesting. Take this photograph of a cuboid construction of large rough-hewn stones built on the high edge of the hillside. Trees surround the man-made intervention. Now, what is the purpose? What would the viewer have this thing be if anything? A gun placement? A sundial? A famous hut overlooking a fjord where a philosopher once wrote in silence?

As I skied along a trail on the western edge of the great glacier I thought of the future. Summer was ending. Anna would be thinking about the new school year. We would soon move to her sister's in Inari even though Anna muttered every year about staying at home. But the summer farm was not made for the winter, however tough the occupants. Birgit had even agreed for Gunnar, our dog, to come with us. Nina and Solveig loved him.

In contrast, marks of irrigation trenches on the surface of the Earth, asteroid impacts on the moon; these are not Girondes. These are tattoos, interesting maybe; but they are things that are and not things that could be.

I had several more photographic assignments planned in the autumn and winter. The landscape was changing here, as it was in other parts of the county. The great glacier was retreating, leaving surprises as it went. The glaciated mountain passes were giving up their hidden treasures as the ice melted. In my pocket was a flat piece of grey metal, mottled in yellow and brown, which I had found on my trip. Was it an arrowhead from a thousand years ago?

The trail of packed snow meandered through small trees and headed down towards a riverbed. Here, I went west to get on to what I called the highway. It was not the most direct route back to the top of the glacier and down the hill to the valley, but it was the most fun. Basically, a long track of packed snow, the highway allowed some high-speed jaunts. The route also avoided some awkward terrain, a zone of crevasses that were tedious to navigate rather than impossible. Skiing fast through the pristine snow of the highway was worth the detour. When skiing, the movement was hypnotic, a comforting long-limbed motion, and a person could truly forget the world.

The highway was open for business with snow blown across it in a herringbone pattern. The Sami had so many words for snow and ice that I made a mental note to ask the word for this design. Across the fishbones were the ski tracks of others who had been this way, and who could blame them; it was like a private flume or toboggan run, with rocks rising to surround the skier. I swished around one bend, shifting my weight to keep speed and direction. I bent down, cocked my poles under my arms, and pretended I was in the Olympics.

When the highway ran out, I slowed around another bend, ready to join a slower path through the trees. I was about to move on, when in the distance, I noticed what appeared to be new debris from the retreating glacier. Moraines, large rocks, and boulders thrown up and discarded by the grinding action of the ice. Rocks were camouflaged in the green and brown khaki of lichen and weathered stone. The glacier was announcing a change; I had to look and investigate. I took off my skies and walked towards the stones. A tunnel suddenly came into view, the entrance through an archway. I followed the white walls towards the blue light and the huge cavern beyond.

What a sight when I walked into that cathedral of ice and colour! A central blue mass of ice rose from the cave floor and spread its wings over me. This feathered canopy was licked yellow and gold from the sun shining through the thin roof of ice. The mythical winged animal, frozen in time, evidently presided over something on the white floor. It was up to me to decide what was being worshipped or protected, and I decided in a flash. Kneeling on the floor, I imagined by own fingers curled around a small sun. The glow would light the black walls and reveal misty streams of water running across the ice-strewn floor. I thought of the sun, then of a candle, then two candles in a candelabra, which made me think of dinner in a restaurant. There and then was born the notion of a surprise anniversary dinner for Anna, to be held in this very place.

The cavern was left over from when the glacier had retreated; the ice had split off forming the tunnel. It seemed safe enough inside. Safer than those caves formed from avalanches, where the snow crashes down the mountain and over time enticing pockets of air form in melting hollows. Such places were traps for hikers looking for interest on the glacier. I was pleased with my find. Ice caves were an easy sell to editors of nature magazines. I decided that I would be back, with the right camera and lenses to set up the shots, and Anna would be with me.

The idea of an anniversary dinner out here in this cavern captured my imagination. We would need a table, and chairs to sit on, plates to eat off. I would need a candelabra, a silver one for twenty-five years together. Other requirements formed quickly. There would be delicious food and wine served on a table with a tablecloth. There would have to be cutlery and wine glasses, although those might be awkward to carry; perhaps goblets would do instead.

Two birds with one stone; I was delighted with this place. There was, however, the possibility that other people would find the cavern and damage it, especially the ice sculpture. I appointed myself its guardian and set about keeping the location secret. I uprooted a short pine tree, nothing more than a sapling, and then used it as a broom, walking backwards away from the cavern to erase my tracks in the snow. Back on the trail I walked a hundred feet away from where I had detoured and built a large pile of rocks to mark the way. The trail dipped at this point, making skiing a pleasure. The route onwards would look much more inviting than a detour into the moraines and the chance of difficult ground. I even stuck the tree in the cairn to make it obvious that this was the way to go.

Life was good. I patted snow off my blue trousers and reattached my long, pointed skies. The country looked beautiful. Tall thin fir trees with feather branches and leaves dotted a wide expanse of white. The way home was marked with ski tracks, old and new. A pine forest bordered the white slopes of a hill that rose to a sky in many shades of blue. Water from my canteen tasted as pure as the air. To live here was a privilege.

It would be good to get home to Anna, as it always had been.

In the early days, I worked long hours. When editors wanted the earth, and would pay little and late, if at all. I was working in Oslo amidst blocks of flats, and other ugly buildings. Anna and I met in Tromsø. She was easily the most gorgeous girl I had ever seen. A teacher and a farmer, she said, which suited an old hippy like me. I said I was a nature photographer, which was how I thought of myself back then.

One more thing about Oslo, worth mentioning. I once saw Mama there when she was a young woman, before she had kids. How was this possible? The young woman who stood in for Mama was looking at herself in a mirror in a shop. She was trying on sunglasses. She looked exactly as Mama would have done when young; the image has never left me.

My room in that house in Oslo was tiny, far too small to entertain Anna. I slept on the top of a bunk bed so I could use the bottom bunk for my equipment. The house was at the end of a row and the subway line ran overhead. It was noisy at first then I tuned it out. There were times when I wondered how I would survive with money, but I did, taking assignments here, there, and everywhere.

I was working near Tromsø one crazy weekend, with three jobs on at once. I was out around the fjords taking shots for the tourist board, while also taking shots on the high grounds of the migrating birds, and, somehow, working on a composition for a competition deadline. I had no time to eat, wash, or look after myself.

Anna came over and found me at the top of a hill. She had cooked a lamb and carrot stew with potatoes, in a metal tin, which she heated up on a camping stove. I was stunned. That was easily the nicest thing anyone had ever done for me. She left me with the food and the rest of that day was easy. I took a rare shot of an eagle feeding its young; that one got a prompt payment. I turned the tourist assignment around and gave the tourists the camera to show me what they were thinking of when they came up the fjords; that one brought me some repeat work. For the competition I shot the fjord, the lush green hills, black and white rocks, the blue and white sky, when all those elements were mirrored in the still water.

Anna was my love and my touchstone. I skied for home, eager to see her and spend the evening thinking about the anniversary surprise. Life for me started with Anna. I kept Mama and Augustin nearby in a cosy gloom, but Anna turned the lights on.

CHAPTER 11

Anna moved on, prodding the way ahead with a walking stick, her Wanderfreunde. For at least an hour, she forced herself to walk forwards and not to look back, not even when she bent down to retie her bootlaces. Down in the valley she saw the homes of her friends painted white. She admired afresh the summer farm which looked better from a distance. Up in the hills, she was cheered up by the sight of purple heather and light green lichen, a reminder of a vacation in Maine. The fjord sparkled and glinted below, the water now emerald green and shining with minerals from the glacier, a precious supply to the wells of the houses and farms around the fjord.

Beyond the sun-dappled peaks she saw the glacier shining in the distance. There were many steep slopes rising from the glistening fjord that proved to be a challenge. At points she slipped on the scree and had to pull handfuls of moss off the rocks as she scrambled her way up. She was kilometres away from the ice, walking through a verdant hillside thick with bushes, birches, and pines, picking her way up the hill to where cascades and cataracts of water began.

Fog drifted over the fjord and the light changed. She was leaving herself behind. The hills bristled with pine trees and the remains of vegetation cleared by avalanches and rockslides. The fjord changed colour: areas became dark like stone, while in other places the waters continued to ripple and reflect the light blue of the sky. She crossed the last road by a small barn and was pleased the owners were not about. In a grove of raspberry bushes, she sat down and picked a handful of fruits and enjoyed them one by one.

Hers would be a difficult trek. She had last been across the glacier with Emil, maybe five years ago. She was tough in a way that was obstinate, but not a thoroughly tough mentality; rather one that was easily broken.

Thoughts of Gunnar intruded. She anticipated the brush

of his big body against her leg, of running her hand through his coat, the touch of his brown nose. She scared herself by imagining that she had buried him in the sheep cairn. The stones of the cairn came away easily when pressed with her mind and fingertips. Black sooty ash blew up into her face when she peeped inside. Gunnar snarled back at her; his canines much longer than she remembered. His gums had receded, the process of decay had set in. She shook her head to clear the image, forcing herself to keep on walking. She had messed up badly, but now was the time to give herself a break and sort things out.

I need help, she thought, and company too. The journey across the glacier was doable in a day but it was difficult. She took out her mobile and rang the glacier school. A voice answered. She asked about the availability of guides, and was in luck, a guide was available at the south-west arm of the mighty glacier. The man on the other end told her mixed weather was expected, but she told him not to worry, that she was well equipped for a day's hike. She gave her DNT membership number and arranged to meet the guide at midday.

It felt good to get away, to start her new life, arranging things on the hoof. Hers would be a trek of solitude for a short while, then she would have some company as the guides took her over the glacier and mountains and pointed her to the coast.

She moved on, and soon the ground grew boggy in places, with larger rocks she slipped on, forcing her to pick her way carefully. At a junction of paths, she followed the route marked with a red T and walked on. One of the DNT huts was nearby, and already her legs had begun to ache.

At the next junction of paths, she realised with a shock where she was and turned off the track. This had been one of their favourite places. They had walked around the narrow lanes and wide tracks of the village, visited the river, found a hidden nature reserve, and admired the beauty of the countryside, all the while wrapped up in each other. The photographer out walking with his pretty girlfriend by his side, bounding along like an overgrown schoolboy, while she alternately quickened and slowed to keep a grasp on his hand.

Emil wore a pair of grey trousers that reminded Anna of the clothes school children wore, material flapping around his ankles. In the winter he liked to pull on a grey jumper his mother had knitted him. But he was no child; he had his serious side. Emil drew meaning from every plant and animal as a magician draws water from a stone.

She sat down on the side of the track under a tree and allowed herself to remember. When they were far away from any buildings and the eyes of the farmers, they kissed. His face would become beatific at such times, as if there were more to her lips than skin and blood. Later on in their courting, they had returned to their special place, guided by the moonlight to an island in the middle of the gushing water, where they made love like nocturnal elves, and in the morning the imprints of their bodies left behind a flattened ring of luxuriant grass.

She reached their special place by a plank bridge over a rushing river supplied by a waterfall that sprayed her as she crossed. She held onto the stripped pine railings as the bridge moved a little. On the other side, a path of mud and tree roots led her to a meadow knee-deep in wildflowers and with a roaring waterfall at its focus. She pulled out a red rubber mat from her rucksack and sat down on it in the thick summer grass. The spray and the noise of the crashing water misted over her face. The sound was tremendous, a continual crashing of water bursting into white foam. They had sat here and been soothed by its constant sound many times. On and on the water poured, cycling from the clouds to the top of the glacier, down through the hills to her special place, where the water ran under her feet and away to the fjord beneath the summer farm.

She wondered what it would have been like to meet herself, twenty years earlier, in this place. What if a young woman with thick blonde hair was sitting next to her now, in a pretty dress, pensive, excited, like a maiden waiting for her knight in a Victorian painting? What would she tell her? That the one she loved was fated to disappear? Would that change her decision to marry him?

The sun struggled at the horizon, and she reckoned the

time to be nearing noon. Here at the edge of the waterfall the white-tipped mountains rose in front of her, and the water-fall cascaded into a peaceful lake. Pure white the water and a fine cloud of spray above it; she could sit all day and watch and listen to its crashing. The sun on her face, the long grasses tickling her head as she lay back in the meadow. Why go on, she would ask her younger self, who would of course have too much energy. This was as good as it gets, and he will always be here; why make it more difficult?

Further minutes passed, and she swapped roles, imagining herself young again, talking with a mysterious traveller, a woman well into middle age, who sat next to her. How old her present self must appear, diminished by life's travails, saddened by the way things had turned out. Her older self would have liked to have appeared wise, but without the gimmick of special knowledge of the young Anna's life ahead. How could she do that? She thought of her mother, and the advice she had been given, and how she had never listened.

With some reluctance, and an aching in the back of her legs, she got up and made her way back to the path. She touched a tall pole planted in the road as she crossed the path. It was four, nearly five, metres high, and last year only its tip had poked out of the snow. Trees had sunk into the earth, houses up to their roofs, the edges of the woods lost beneath the snow. Fridtjof was right: one could be forgotten up here for weeks in bad weather. But last year, in the flattest places, when the snowfall had been whipped up like meringues, she had appreciated the beauty of the place.

At the next junction, the red T on the fencepost pointed her across a meadow, and she knew she was near the hiking hut. She strode on, her brown leather walking boots blazing a trail through the heather. A second wind filled her body: her thoughts of grief and regret were clearing. She was on the way to solving the mystery of Emil's non-existence, and as she walked, she allowed Gunnar to run happily along by her side.

The hiking hut appeared, a long grey building with wooden plank walls supported on stones, and a turfed roof for insulation. She went up the steps to the front door at the end of the building and took out her key.

CHAPTER 12

Anna was cooking dinner while I turned the image of the ice cathedral over in my mind. I hummed a tune as I paced around the farmhouse.

'You're happy,' she said.

'Of course. I'm with you.'

The school dance: holding her close, that long guitar solo winding around us.

We kissed. 'You're up to something,' she said.

I was ready for questions, so I went over to the wall and adjusted an old photograph for which I had won a prize. A cart drawn by a donkey; three people, the native driver, myself and Augustin; tourists in Algeria. I had my arms around Augustin and the driver, and the purple of my long-sleeved shirt was so intense it focussed the picture perfectly.

'You're right, I am working on something. Two remarkably interesting buildings, I must show you some time.'

'I look forward to it,' she said. There was a knock at the door. Yvonne, a teacher colleague of Anna's was outside, crying. Anna took her away to sit in the living room where she tried to calm and comfort her. I was supposed not to hear their conversation, but I did.

'You still hold hands!' exclaimed Yvonne, who immediately quietened down, so I had to step nearer the door to listen.

'It's true, we still hold hands. We won the lottery with our very first ticket. We even hold hands in bed.' Anna laughed.

'You never fight!' This statement came later after a great deal of sobbing.

I moved away. Of course, we do not fight, we have seen enough fighting. Dad throwing the dog across the room when I was young was a moment never to be forgotten.

'You let one another speak, and never do the other down.' The door had swung open a little now and Yvonne was in full flow. 'You always talk nicely to each other!'

I pottered about in the kitchen, turning over the mottled

piece of ironwork I had found on the ice. Perhaps an arrow-head from the Vikings, or maybe something much more mundane, something to do with farming and only fifty years old? The ice was teasing us, showing its mysteries and memories at random.

I took a walk outside to ponder the proposed set-up in the cavern. Essentially it would be an anniversary dinner set at a restaurant table. The trouble would be to bring a table all the way out there. I thought of asking Siegfried or Petter to help, but then I thought again. There was no need to bring a table out there at all. I would build a table from whatever stones and rocks I could find. As for chairs, who needed them anyway? I would borrow a couple of hassocks from the church at the edge of the fjord. We would kneel and face each other across the roughly hewn altar. The act of worship seemed appropriate for the occasion. I would also bring our best white tablecloth; there were no high days coming up so Anna would not miss it.

Hassocks, tablecloth, and what about the centrepiece: the sun in the eagle's claws? A suitable candelabra would have to be sourced. What would we eat and drink? We were known in the area for our brunost, a brown cheese made from goats' milk and with the taste of caramel and fudge. It was excellent with bread and ham, or roasted goat kid, yet these were staples we had on a daily or weekly basis. One of the greatest tastes Anna and I enjoyed in our early days was foie gras with a dessert wine from Monbazillac. I would need to go into Tromsø to find such delicacies.

There would have to be an anniversary present as well. I had taken more notice of what she wore today: small silver stud earrings and a silver bracelet. She caught me noticing these items and had smiled. We have been together a long time.

Anna was still talking with Yvonne. I picked up a small rucksack and torch and walked down to the fjord with my Hasselblad, watching the shadows on the water in the gathering gloom. The church was cold inside, and the medieval trappings made it a much more foreboding place, where the ideas of demons and ghosts became stronger. I walked down the nave, eager not to bump into the ends of the pews or touch any part of the place. Light from my torch flitted across the altar set back in its recess. Five candles stood in the candelabra on the white cloth. There was the sound of creatures rustling in the dark. My boot kicked the altar rail and made me stop short. Behind the altar, a man and a woman looked down, and in the middle, Christ hung on the cross.

Each pew had hassocks neatly laid out on the wooden benches. These were personal hassocks often made and sewn by families for one another. I didn't want to steal; I wanted to borrow. Behind the altar, was a frieze, framed in golden scrollwork, and behind that the door to the vestry. I pushed the cold metal of the door and then tugged, but it did not move. Of course, the vestry was locked, and for good reason; there was a risk of the ornaments being stolen, as I was about to prove.

I saw what was needed, in a box by the alter; several old hassocks, faded and fraying, waiting for repair. I placed two of the best-looking into the rucksack. If Fridtjof was to see me now, he would think me a common thief. But Fridtjof was a blabbermouth; he couldn't be trusted with the secret of a surprise anniversary dinner. Anna would only have to look at him once to realise something was up.

I lifted the flap of another box. Rows of white candles lay neatly packed. There was the wonderful smell of lanolin and the dust from the altar. Now things were worse; borrowing had become stealing as I placed two candles in my rucksack. Fridtjof might have a point about Anna's husband, a man who never darkened the church doors, who came and went to suit himself. I packed the box of candles up, returning each flap to its original position.

The door of the church opened behind me. In a flash, I had the Hasselblad up to my eye as if composing a shot of the altar. Tuva, Steinar's wife, called out a greeting. She was delivering flowers to the church.

'Sorry,' she said. 'are you taking a photograph?'

'Thinking about it, but I've never been one for religious iconography. I like our church, and the flowers of course, but I can never look at him.' I pointed to the image of Christ on the cross. 'It is too awful. How can people worship the image of a dying man on a wooden cross with nails through his hands and feet?'

Tuva put bunches of flowers in vases either side of the chancel. 'I agree. In some churches it's even worse.'

I helped her with flowers for other vases. 'The biggest shock I ever had was when I was walking in Italy, climbing the via ferrata in the Dolomites. I was walking down a narrow street in Trentino, passing doorways into shops selling trinkets and bric-a-brac to the tourists, when I came across a display of crucifixes. Some were taller than you, much bigger than life-size. I had to walk past them, and the largest one, I can see it now, a huge crown of thorns on his head. Well, it was horrible. I tried to walk by, but the figure's eyelids rolled back, and I could see his painted eyes. I leapt out of my skin and fell over pictures and paintings in the passageway. I had to pretend to an angry shopkeeper that I had been stung by a wasp.'

Tuva laughed and looked up at the cross. 'You'd think he really was alive.'

I helped Tuva a while longer with the flowers, before taking my leave and picking up my rucksack and stolen goods. People do strange things when they are in love, that is for sure. Robbing a church was a low point. I stubbed my shoe on the end of a pew as I left. Tuva smiled and wished me well.

After dinner, Anna and I sat on the sofa and watched the latest hit TV show. The Hurtigruten ferry was making the journey from Bergen, in the south of Norway, to Kirkenes in the north, close to the border with Russia. The voyage would take an estimated one hundred and thirty-four hours and it would be televised in real time. I was mesmerised by the prow of the boat gliding through the never-ending sea. As the ship left Bergen, a flotilla of small boats buzzed around it like Daphnia in a pond. Anna fell asleep. I watched until the early hours and listened to Gunnar snoring in his basket in the kitchen. Slow TV was a hit in our household but only with me.

In the morning I was up early before Anna even stirred. I walked down the track with my rucksack on my back and caught the bus from Burfjord to Tromsø. The Monbazillac was easily obtained. I had to look far harder to find the animal-friendly foie gras Anna would insist on, but I eventually found a can in the food hall of a department store. They also had a candelabra and a tablecloth, shorter than the one at home, and easier to pack. The candelabra was perfect, with a short thick stem, even thicker base, and two side shoots for candles. At a jeweller, once recommended to me by a magazine editor, I found the perfect present for Anna.

Back at the farm I considered a suitable hiding place for the items I had bought. Anna was not averse to unpacking my rucksack, so I needed to be careful. There were several outbuildings; the goat shed seemed appealing, although Anna spent a lot of time in there. Perhaps the cool shed would be better, where she made the cheese. I walked around the farm and considered the newly built sheep cairn, but that was rather macabre. Fancy finding a candelabra in amongst the funeral stones. In the end I brought in enough logs from under the lean-to to leave a space at the back for a box with all the goodies hidden within. I kept Anna's special present hidden in an old camera case, such was my paranoia.

At the end of that momentous day, as she lay asleep next to me, I turned the image of our place of worship over in my mind again and considered its impact on the viewer. We would discover, as if by accident, the route to the cavern. Then I would lead Anna into that hall of ice where the sight of the glowing candelabra grasped in the eagle's feet would do the rest.

CHAPTER 13

'I t's open,' called a voice from inside. A man appeared at the door of the cabin. He was younger than her, about forty she guessed, with dark brown almost black hair flecked with some grey around the edges. He had wide, slightly puffy eyes and an engaging smile. His chest was broad under a red and black T-shirt.

'I hoped I'd see someone up here. I've been here for a night. Wondered if anyone else would be about.'

She entered the hiking cabin, a warm and clean space panelled throughout in pine wood. The bathroom had a plastic toilet, metal sink, a pitcher of water. Rooms full of bunk beds that slept forty. Suddenly she felt tired.

'I'm Tomas,' the man said. 'I'm making some hot chocolate. Would you like some?'

'Thank you.'

'Are you hungry? I'm starving.'

She nodded. 'Yes, I am.'

'I'll fix something,' he said. He returned to the stove and stirred milk and chocolate powder into a pan. In two other pans, he poured pasta shells into boiling water, and into another he emptied a tin of pasta sauce. The list of foods used were noted on a piece of paper with his name and membership number and placed in the payments box.

She was resting on a seat when he brought her a white mug of hot chocolate and sat down opposite her. She cradled the mug in her hands and tasted the sweet liquid.

'Wonderful,' she said.

There was a doll on the table, a troll with wild grey hair, red jacket, a striped skirt, and large gypsy earrings. She picked it up. The troll had three eyes, four fingers on each hand, and a long, crooked nose. A red walking stick in one hand reminded travellers who they might meet on their journeys. Anna smoothed the skirt and replaced the troll on the table.

Tomas smiled and drank from his cup. 'Where are you

59

headed?'

'The glacier, and then the coast, to Uektefjord.'

'Uektefjord, you say?'

Anna nodded. 'Do you know it?'

'I've just come from there on an assignment. I'm a journalist, working for *Folkebladet*.'

'You went over the glacier?'

'Yes, I had a good guide. His name was Lars. A young man, straight out of the glacier school but very competent.'

'I remember that school. It took two weeks to pass as a glacier guide.'

'It's one week now, I hear.' Tomas smiled, and the lines creased around his eyes. 'Lars was good company; we had no trouble.'

'How long did it take?'

'A long day, I was tired at the end, but happy.' He drained his drink. 'You're going to Uektefjord, that's interesting. To meet the guru?'

She held the mug of hot chocolate to her lips. 'Who?'

Tomas laughed. 'Well, that's my name for him, he's not really a guru, but some people call him that.'

'Who is this person? I'm intrigued.'

'His name is Berkeley Ritz, Berkeley as in California, and Ritz as in the hotel in London. He's an English philosopher, a bit of a celebrity.'

'The funny thing is, I never got to meet him. He's got a second-in-command, a man called Martin, who was helpful.'

'What were his followers like? Were they academics?'

'No, most of his audience were tourists, hopping off the boats as they go up and down the coast, but many stay a week at the hotel. Well, it looks like a hotel, it's a private villa really.' Tomas shook his head. 'They're so funny. They say they have invented a utopia for themselves.'

'A utopia?' She considered the word. 'If only.'

'Or at least a beautiful place. People go there to watch the sunset, to sit and think, and talk, so much talking.'

Anna sat up. Emil would have loved such a place.

Tomas suddenly remembered his cooking and darted back to the kitchen. Anna heard him removing pans from the stove and the clink, clink of plating up food.

'So, they're like summer people, with the second home in the country.'

'Exactly. They meet in a place of natural wonder, which fits their ideals perfectly.'

Tomas presented her with a steaming bowl of pasta and tomato sauce. 'They call the place Hyperborea, after the Greek myth: a land of plenty and harmony, situated beyond Boreas, the north wind.'

Anna tasted her pasta, which was delicious and too hot. 'It's true that it's warmer here now, even on the coast. But what do they do there, apart from talk?'

'They say they're looking for the Good, with a capital G, and draw inspiration from people who do good. They meet throughout the year.'

'Ah,' she said, and she looked at the doll on the table. 'And do they also worship crystals, or hide from trolls?'

'I went looking for all of that but found nothing. No objects were worshipped, they had no services as you would in a church, just group meetings. I was there four days and waited for them to do something crazy, something to titillate my readers, but they turned out to be very hospitable, even charming.' He laughed again. 'You know, when I first met them, I did think that I'd walked into a church meeting. There were so many old couples there, grey heads, men and women together, some older women on their own, but also some youngsters, some clever-looking men and women, university types.'

'They don't sound so bad.'

'They were fine, absolutely OK, completely benign. Many different nationalities, not exactly a rainbow coalition, but close.'

They continued to eat their meal together, Anna feeling more and more relaxed.

'If they're tourists,' she said, 'they must be careful not to outstay their welcome, even in our relaxed country.'

'They stay only for a week or two in the summer, until the midnight sun disappears.' Tomas put down his fork leaving a cleared plate. 'They call themselves The Assembly.'

Now Anna laughed. 'I can relate to that. I'm a school-teacher. In our assemblies we all sit together, children with teachers. It's a nice way of doing things.'

'If not the assembly, what takes you to Uektefjord?' Tomas cleared away the plates, and Anna was pleased to have some space to herself while he busied away in the kitchen.

'I'm visiting family.' She tensed as she said the lie, not because she thought that Tomas needed to know the truth, but it occurred to her she was not even sure where she would stay tonight.

'Well, maybe you'll meet some of these guys. They live in a beautiful villa built by Ritz, evidently a rich man. Maybe they can help all of us to live well together.'

Anna stood up and looked out through the windows. Now she was mindful of the time, and of her arrangement to meet the guide. 'We live well, don't we, in the Finnmark? Look at our toll payments for the roads, or how the DNT organise these huts. All based on honesty. And then there are the Sami, who we let live their traditional ways or join us in modern society as they please.'

Tomas came back out of the kitchen. 'Perhaps that's why the tourists chose Uektefjord for their spot. It's warm and peaceful, and the fjord is beautiful.' He opened a notebook. 'Let me see. Hyperborea was a place of beauty, with two harvests a year and people living in harmony, beyond the north wind. It was the furthest place north on the map.'

'But a myth, you said?'

'Of course: a myth, an ideal, an escape. A place away from it all, no intruders, no attackers to invade your country. Like the Elysian fields, except of course that everyone is alive.' Tomas started to slice a pear in pieces. 'Would you like some?'

She shook her head. 'It's like the Norse invasions again, except in reverse, with the English having their turn at trying some new philosophy out in a new land.'

'That's a good idea,' said Tomas, and he wrote in his notebook. 'I hadn't thought of that. They meet in the cold pure north, and, by all accounts, live to help others. It's a human rights organisation, I suppose. You'll be able to read all about it when I get back to Tromsø. Are you sure you don't want some pear, or an apple?'

It would be so easy to stay, she thought. Stay and talk to this interesting man. Choose a bunk and a duvet from the stores. Take out the cotton sleeping bag she had packed and stay the night. But she had booked the guide, and she needed to get going.

'Thank you, no. I have a long way to go, but I will take some chocolate bars if there are any, and some raisins.'

'Of course.' Tomas got up and found three chocolate bars in the store cupboard and placed them on the table. 'Look, have these as well. I made some for myself and I have too much to carry.' Tomas placed some sandwiches wrapped in grease-proof paper in her bag. 'It was nice to meet you.'

'You too.' She struggled on with her backpack. 'What route did you take?'

'Over Stortfjell and Litefjell, and down a valley to Uek-tefjord. Watch out for the weather. It can be good one moment, and bad the next.'

'It's OK, I'm used to it.'

Tomas looked out of the window. 'I'll have to get a move on when I've written my piece up.' He rubbed the stubble on his chin as he inspected the clouds. 'You may get some raindrops on your hike.'

'It's nothing.'

She left Tomas with a wave goodbye at the door of the hut, and with a promise to read his article. The trail took her up into the mountain plains, where the sky was grey and dimly lit on the horizon. She made a call to a number that had remained in her phone for three years. The proprietor of the hotel in Uektefjord answered. They had a room available; she made the reservation for tonight. With her imagination racing, she imagined Emil in a room on a villa set on a beach, camera pointed at the sun.

Her legs ceased to ache, and she strode on.

CHAPTER 14

There was the shock as we cried out together and then the laughter. I fell softly down on her, cradling her head, kissing her lips. We looked up into the mirror fixed on the ceiling above the bed. The border was decorated with hearts and pitchforks, just like the rocking chair. We smiled and pulled faces as if they were in a photo booth. Then we plumped up the pillows and sat up for a while holding hands.

'You are happy today,' she said. 'Very much stronger, like when you were young.' She kissed me on the cheek.

'Yes, I feel young. I will take a trip up on to the glacier. I want to photograph those old farm buildings today. They will make a good picture.'

'Oh, I thought it might be because of something else.'

'I cannot complain; my situation is excellent.'

She kissed me again, got up, and I admired her long supple legs, that I had once likened to frog's legs, even calling her froggy once as she gripped me in bed.

Midway through the morning Anna brought me my phone. My brother, Augustin, had texted. 'He has a title fight in Oslo. Do we want tickets? I've checked your diary; we are free on the date.'

'OK, book us in.' Augustin in the ring, arms aloft, his smiling sweating face, mouthguard protruding. An enormous golden buckle on his belt. He was the champ. I was never troubled by the toughs at school. How I came to have a brother like him was one of nature's mysteries.

There is a photograph of all four of us. Papa, Mama, Augustin and me. I was too young to remember Papa much. But I do remember Augustin raging in our bedroom. Papa had not come back. He really had gone this time. Augustin bought a punching bag and drew his face on it. He knocked the stuffing out of it for days. Eventually, he calmed down and joined a gym. After anger comes acceptance said Mama.

I worked for most of the afternoon, in a room that made

a fair workshop. Anna came in. 'I made you these today.' I offered her the small black box in my hand.

Anna's eyes were bright as she took the box and brushed her fingers over the velvet cover. Inside the box was a pair of silver earrings, shaped like leaves, presented on a cushion of black felt. She held one of the earrings up to the light. I could see that she liked them.

She went to the mirror and fixed them in her ears. I put my arms around her, and we kissed.

'Let's dance,' I said. I took hold of her, wrapped her in my arms, and hugged her to me. We danced together to an old tune on the radio, at first shifting around in circles, and then slowly warming up to the beat as our body heat increased.

I crooned in her ear, and she responded. 'Do you have a car? That would be great, we could drive into Tromsø.'

I shook my head. 'I love you.'

The song changed to another hit.

'Everything will be all right,' I sang.

Our dancing evolved: Anna and I spun and shimmied through the next few songs, until the cold was forgotten. Then 'The Word' came on.

I recited the lyrics.

'That's nice,' she laughed, as my hands moved up and down her back. 'Now I'm hot; I'm sweating.'

'The album is called Rubber Soul - rubbery soul. I've always loved that.'

She nudged me along. 'It is the end to a perfect day.'

'One of the best,' I replied, 'when we know that everything's going to be all right.'

'You're wonderful, Emil. You have such a wonderful optimism.'

She saw me glance at the pink skin under her shirt, then to her new earrings. 'It's because I'm with you,' I said, kissing her again. The candlelight played on her hair, inviting my touch and taste.

She placed her hot hands on my head and brushed the hair out of my eyes. I lost myself in her green eyes, piercing emeralds. She was between me and a lamp on a wall, and the light framed her head in a bright glow. Our bodies relaxed into one another, mouths searching for lips. I felt goose bumps bristle on my arms. My ardour was raised, and she pressed into it.

'Now would be good,' she said.

We waltzed from the living room to the bedroom, bumping off the furniture and on to the bed. She sat up while I pulled off her top, and she took off my tunic. We stripped further, and then we sat before each other. We looked up at our reflections in the mirror. 'We look like statues.'

'I need a suntan.' Then I grasped her bottom, made her shout, and dug my nails into her flesh. My erection pushed up between our bellies; her nipples were like dark moles on her chest. We slipped underneath the bedclothes and howled at the touch of the cold sheet, rubbing our bodies together until we were warm again. Anna stretched out her butterscotch body, glowing in the candlelight. I attended to her, stroking her skin, like a sculptor over a bronze nude. Then we moulded and joined and melded our bare skin into a new animal that rocked up and down until it eventually roared and separated into two figures again.

'Lovely,' she breathed.

'Wonderful. You are wonderful.'

Later, I dressed and got ready for my day trip. Three days to our anniversary; I wanted everything to be perfect. While Anna milked the goats, I retrieved the items hidden in the wood pile, and checked her gift was still in the camera case.

'I will be back for dinner, and more of the Hurtigruten journey; it's quite gripping in an extremely slow way. The boat will reach Ålesund today.'

She smiled. 'I will prepare some lessons and keep you company.'

We kissed, and it was like one of the kisses when we first met, looking into each other's eyes.

'You are young again.' She brushed back my hair. 'I like it.'

I hoisted up my rucksack and thought gleefully about my plan. What a day this would be. I swear the kiss we shared in the kitchen doorway before I set off tasted of orange sherbet. I set off, looking back at Anna to wave at every opportunity, walking into the trees like a clown. Finally, I was out of sight of the farm and heading up the hill and eventually to the glacier.

The going was easy. I recognised the waypoints I needed and made good progress. After several hours walking, I noticed something new in the distance: a standing stone, four metres high, its surface all the shades of grey and white. The stone had a flat front and back, and thin sides. It was almost a rectangle but there had been a deliberate working to suggest a head, torso and legs. It was sunk in the ground so that the earth reached up around its base to support it. The stone was a watcher on the way. I knew no-one in the area capable of such a construction; there was another artist about.

Being out on the ice helped me to think about the stone as a mirror; a Rosetta stone to learn from. The ominous and sinister: one man's standing stone is another man's waymarking guardian. I projected myself on to that watching figure, and it became my protector, not a highwayman.

I continued taking the tough route to the glacier, passing several places I knew well from travelling with Anna. Eventually I found the track near the ice cavern. The tree was still there, sticking out of the stones, pointing hikers and skiers down the highway. I detoured off the compressed snow and over to the moraines in the distance.

The ice tunnel shone blue and led me to the cavern beyond, like ultraviolet lines on a flower leading a bee to nectar. The sight of the enormous ice eagle was a forgotten shock. The massive creature rose and spread its wings over me. I surveyed the interior. In the furthest darkest corners, there was the sound of water dripping on to the floor like the high notes on a piano. Drips of water also fell on my head at points from holes in the cave roof as I walked across the floor to the magnificent structure of the giant eagle, blue wings tinged with the colours of the rainbow.

The table was built using a selection of rocks brought in from outside. Manhandling the rocks was hot, difficult work. When I looked at my watch, two hours had passed. In the end, I fashioned a rocky cube, slightly taller than my knee, and wider than my shoulders. The table had a tolerably flat surface on which to put plates, cutlery, and goblets.

I noticed that the cavern floor was wet from ice melting

from the walls. This would mean that the hassocks would also be wet unless they were placed on dry stones, another puzzle that took longer than anticipated to solve. The wind had got up and was singing by the time I had finished and stepped back to survey the work. The table looked like a short chimney stack with two hassocks at each side. Anna's hassock was maroon with blue diamonds, while mine was chequered in yellow and brown.

I unpacked the candelabra and placed it on the rocky table. This was going to be good. I lit the two candles and stood back. The golden sun appeared in the cavern under the eagle's claws. It was just as I had imagined it.

A lump of ice fell from the cave roof and landed behind me. I waited but there were no more surprises. The wind gusted and I noticed its warmth. Men do crazy things to impress a woman. I unpacked two white plates and two knives. At the darkest reach of the cavern, out of the way of the warming sun, I scooped out a hole in the ground big enough to hold the package of foie gras, flatbreads, goblets, and bottle of Monbazillac, all wrapped up in the new white tablecloth.

The table was set. The food would be served on white plates and we would each have a knife to spread the faux foie gras on flatbreads. The new goblets, the best of modern pottery, had been easiest to pack with the Monbazillac. The lit candelabra was magnificent. My stomach rumbled from excitement at the thought of the meal and the look on Anna's face.

Then the stone under my brown and yellow hassock shifted a little and sunk a little lower into the melting ice floor. Water streamed around it. The rocky table tilted a little from the horizontal and put the question to all my good work.

CHAPTER 15

After an hour's walking Anna's pace had slowed again. She stopped to find some bilberries and blueberries to nibble on. Every time a sheep jinked out of the way and its bell tinkled with the trudge of her feet on the track, her thoughts turned to Gunnar. The terrain rose higher and the leaves on the bilberries turned red. In one spot of low-growing bushes, she was delighted to find some cloudberries, yellow fruits like raspberries but with larger sacs and only a tinge of red at the top. She popped a few in her mouth. They tasted like apricots, or, as she liked to think, the sun.

Now the way ahead changed. She smelt the mountain grasses and a fragrance like thyme drifted across her path. Grouse dappled in grey and white watched her pass, hidden in the colour of the rocks, their hooting like laughter. What appeared to be tufts of sheep's wool caught on flowers were cotton plants growing on the plain.

She stood still and listened to the birds, the sun on her face. In the silence, she heard water melting from the glacier. There would be a stream soon, and then a river. She moved on, following the path which began to wind upwards around the valley wall. The path narrowed at points, and she had to hold on to the rock face to keep her footing. The sound of rushing water grew louder, the cool air turned moist. Soon water was running past her feet. She found a shallow place and waded across, keeping her balance with her stick. When she was across, she was pleased to find her boots were still dry, and she carried on upstream, the river growing beside her in speed and whiteness. It marked the way ahead. The point of her walking stick found the firm ground and set off.

Sometime later she found old horse tracks that lost their shape quickly when interrogated with her walking stick. She carried on, feeling the tightness return to the backs of her legs. Her face was hot, so she drank from her water bottle and told herself off for being weak; plenty of women her age walked or skied these distances, and she needed to shape up. She imagined her face was glowing red like the fire she had lit under Gunnar; she winced at the image. The flames had not lasted long. She was blanking the memory of a big sack full of white powder that came next.

The whiteness of the mountains pulsed with the unexpected heat of the sun. She tipped some lotion on to her hand, rubbed it in to her skin. Her mobile phone had reception; she was not completely alone. Moreover, she had a clue to Emil's disappearance, if not an actual lead. No one had ever mentioned a villa full of sun-loving philosophers before.

The ground now became broken, split into rocks strewn like debris across the grass or sunk into dips where lakes reflected the sky like mirrors. At this altitude, the mountain ranges looked like islands strung out in a chain, snow and ice merging into mist and fog, touching the white clouds in the bright blue sky.

The lake widened, rocky piers grew out into its depths, and a road appeared on her right, running along the water's edge. Beyond the lake, the glacier glistened on the top of the mountain, like white paint spilt into a bowl.

The horse tracks disappeared at the road's edge. She followed the tarmac, lined with high poles, until a sign directed her off the path towards the glacier's arm. The light from the low sun faded and the sky became darker, the air misty, as she crunched over small stones and walked around giant boulders. She was walking back in time, chasing the path along which the glacier had crawled thousands of years ago. Her stick poked at rough markings in the brown ground scraped clean of vegetation by the retreating ice. She walked on for a hundred metres, over clear, flat, gouged land, small rivers meeting her path, their dirty whiteness melting into the lake behind her.

The way ahead ascended gradually, and Anna noticed her breathing grow noisy. She looked up and saw a finger of the glacier creep over the rock and hang in blue and white, enticing her forward. Her path was well-worn, and she assumed she was on the path up towards the glacier. Crushed and cracked rocks marked the edge of the glacier's slow slide;

dirty rocks, browns and blacks, broken into pieces where the glacier had crawled. Then the rocks became smaller, more whites than browns, in beds washed clean by the foaming river water, and soon all the way ahead was white.

And then, quite suddenly, the edge of the lake returned, and she stood at the tip of the glacier's tongue, beneath an ice wall stretching metres above her. It looked like a giant bear's paw, with fingers and nails. She patted the ice with her gloved hand. A giant, she thought, as in the tales of old. She investigated the deep inky-blue wells in the icy creases and holes. She had not been on a glacier for years, and had forgotten the depth of blue, shades from the colour of duck eggs to dense indigo. Sitting down on her mat, she fixed crampons over her boots and tied them on. The metal teeth that gripped the ice gave her confidence to climb up a shallow slope onto the glacier. There were certain places to enter a glacier with safety: one had to find the correct arm to cross on, one without crevasses.

She climbed up on the ice, her gloved hands giving her purchase. After a few steps, the feeling of walking on ice came back to her. Water ran on the surface, which crunched under her crampons but did not trouble the metal teeth of her shoes. When draughts of hot air gusted off the ice, the thermal currents brought back memories of hikes with Emil. There was no sign of her guide or anyone else. She sat down on her red mat and unpacked Tomas's sandwiches: salami and cucumber in one, pickled herring and egg in another. An apple and banana in the bag too. The kindness of strangers, she thought; she liked the idea, but was glad she was getting away. Fridtjof had tried to be a good friend to her, but he was too conventional for her tastes. Where was the freedom of human expression, she saw in the schoolchildren's play? Why did everyone have to fit in? What about the eccentrics? To disperse into the wilds was her wont, her nature, and she could not quell the need to get away.

Tumbling waterfalls pouted silvery tracks of water down the mountain sides around her; she likened them to snails' trails. In the distance ahead and above her the plain of white ice stretched away towards the peaks of Stortfjell and Litefjell. There were many dangers: small crevasses with beguiling blue walls and deep bottoms, easy to step over if you were awake, and easy to step into if you were asleep. Folds in the ice threw up stairways to walk on if you watched your step.

When she heard feet crunch on the ice, she stood expecting her guide, but the first body turned into two, and then became a group of four teenagers, jolly youngsters who danced around the bore holes, the moulins, that dropped tens of metres to the very bottom of the ice. Anna tensed when the kids looked into these holes: they were death-traps that could take a person to the bottom of the glacier and keep them there for a lifetime, returning the body a hundred years later, if at all. But the teenagers were careful; they waved at her, and she waved back.

The kids moved on to an ice corridor, shrieking as they squeezed between two blue ice walls as they became, temporarily, the ice cubes in an ice cube maker. Then they settled down on the rim of a bowl, looking down the glacier, and pulled out their lunch. She made a quick inventory of her equipment: she wore sunglasses, sun-cream, ear protection from the wind. A nutritious lunch had been consumed; there was chocolate and raisins as an emergency ration. The children, two teenage boys sprouting wild hair on their heads, two teenage girls with hair in buns, wore normal clothes, boots but no crampons, and were unprotected from the sun in t shirts and coats open to the elements. Between them they shared sandwiches out of plastic packets. She waved and got their attention, holding up an offer of her water bottle; they waved back and held up cans of coca cola.

The colour of the ice brightened when she took off her sunglasses. Her world became more real, and dirtier in its details. A black oily residue like dirt or pollution of some kind covered the large ice crystals, full of air, which crunched and split under crampons. She rubbed some of the dirt between her fingers; it stained them black, the remains of animals dead for millennia, giving a grey and black crust to the ice, which cleared as she looked deeper and then became amazing shades of blue. The glacier stretched away into the distance, its gleaming slopes climbing higher towards the sky.

Emil, she thought, if you are out there, try and make it a little easier for me to find you.

CHAPTER 16

I started to pack up my rucksack with the realisation that I had been foolish, I would need to abort the plan. There was no heat brighter than the flame of our love, but this was a dangerous way of celebrating it. There was heat and white light from the two bright flames of the candles, and the love of ice for heat is well established. Oh, Anna, if you could have only seen this place, you would have loved it. An inviting but temporary cavern, a deadly Venus fly trap, and I would have brought you here.

I hurried to pack away my camera when the first chunks of ice started to fall around me. I looked up and saw that the ice eagle had lurched forward with its wings scraping the ground. In the moment that I registered the dismay of the fallen eagle, larger pieces of ice began to rain on my head. The eagle collapsed into huge sections of ice and the rainbow vanished from its wings.

I tried to run to the entrance, but I lost my footing. I put out my hands as I went down and cut them on hidden rocks, smashing my knee. Above me the sun shone through the new holes in the roof. The warmth from the sky reached down for the candelabra that laid on its side with candles extinguished. Larger chunks of ice fell and crashed on to the floor. I curled up at the base of the destroyed eagle, face stricken, hands up, warding off the falling ice.

The roof was giving way. The sun entered the cavern, eager to connect with the heat from the miniature star within. The image of the sun through the roof was clear; I remember it as I speak now. Then there was a shift of the camera to a new scene. I was flat on my back with ice and snow on my chest. My vision was doing something quite peculiar, repeatedly scrolling upwards to the collapsed roof. I could not control it. I moaned and groaned, trying to clear this unpleasant experience. My breathing was shallow; I could not move or take a full breath. There was mist rising around me, meltwater trickling past my inert body, draining into several holes in the cavern floor.

A man-high chunk of ice lay next to me; it must have been the capstone of the cavern. I surmised that I had been knocked flat by it and that it had broken apart around me. There was black sediment on the ice, which would have trapped the sunlight and encouraged melting and collapse. Parts of the walls of the cavern were pushed outwards and now seemed thin and insubstantial. The weight of the roof must have been too much in the end.

I could only breath softly and take it all in. Water was streaming down any walls still standing. The rocky table lay in ruins, the tablecloth a sodden besmirched mess. There were some remains of the opening arch, but little else. The ice eagle was no more, its body and wings separated on the floor. A shard of blue ice rimmed with gold lay beside me. Was the gold a trick of the light or a valuable mineral?

I was moving. Even with my damaged senses, I could tell that I was slowly sliding downstream from the smashed eagle to the darkest regions of the cavern. There was the sound of running water to accompany me being carried along by the melting ice to an unknown destination. I could do little to resist. I was soaked through and getting colder by the moment, sliding along the wet cavern floor with a sickening feeling of vertigo.

I lay for what seemed like hours, watching the sun continue its arc across the sky. My beer can camera on the roof of the summer farm was set to record the passage of Apollo's chariot. Would Anna develop the film now that I was leaving and would not be back home? Did she even know that the camera was there?

I needed to make one last image before the inevitable: a farewell message on my phone. My camera was in its waterproof enclosure next to the candelabra. My phone was next to me, screen smashed, display dark. I would like to leave something for you Anna, to make sure that you know I was alright at the end. There is a permanent marker pen in my pocket, for labelling film cassettes. The top comes off and falls on to the ice, but no matter, I have a firm grip on the pen. There;

I have recorded my last message as best I can; the only thing that I need to say, with a shaking hand and not much time left.

Emil Gironde studied photography in Oslo and worked as an associate photographer for several wildlife and nature magazines. Influenced by imagist poets, Hulme, Pound, etc, his early work concentrated on images of juxtaposed complementary colours found in nature. He changed direction in later life to photograph exterior artefacts, notably buildings, in monochrome. His publications include *Red Bird, Green Leaves (2012)* and *Shade and Shadow* (2018).

This was not going to end well. I closed my eyes, but the sliding sensation remained. I was on a conveyor belt in a crematorium. The door would open to allow the coffin through, and then it would close, and that would be that. I knew that I was dreaming, that I was somewhere in a darkened place struggling to wake up. I was hanging on, reaching out a hand, waiting to be picked up, waiting for someone to appear by my side. There was no-one about. The ice cave was not on an obvious route across the glacier. It had taken a detour to get here, and I had done well to dissuade any likeminded explorers.

I remembered a postcard, hand sized and glossy, with a scene of a river and a background of fir trees. A young man and woman were in a boat, dressed in funny costumes, light suede jackets with tassels, each held a paddle out of the water.

The thrill of the present predicament and the mysterious object from the past.

That postcard was on my bedside cupboard for ages. The click of the cupboard door, the smell of wood, and of chocolate mints hidden inside. The click of the door closing. Secrets. The development of personality.

Keep track. Keep focus.

They were Indians in a canoe carved from a tree. On the back of the card was a red maple leaf. Greetings from Canada. The scrawl was hard to read. I could only make out the name. Uncle Conrad on the bottom line. One of two mysterious uncles never seen. Should I have shown it to Maman and Augustin or keep it secret? Deception. A message from another world. Excitement. A world that I wish to visit. Indians. Native Americans. Tanned faces. Exotica. The open sea. The future.

A second postcard arrived at some point in my childhood. From Poland! In a forest, two young people wearing coats were escaping into the trees. Both had shaved heads, were barefoot and wore dark grey blankets. The young woman was further up the tree than the man. They turned around just at the right time to be captured by the photographer. It was an artfully posed shot. Chests, nipples, not an ounce of fat. There was a stillness and patience about the actors that belied the supposed urgency in their escape. Still, the photographer did a good job and got his shot away.

There is the trumpet solo again. Anna hears it; and I hear her. I am sliding on an icy floor towards a meltwater hole in a cave. Close your eyes and feel for the image and words, pour out what you feel. A building that says something because you are mouthing the words.

This collapsed cave says the end of Emil.

Early Girondes were easy to spot. They sold in the front windows of art galleries in the cities. A yellow sunset against the purple sea. An orange tulip against the blue sky. A red bird amongst the green leaves. Yes, those were early Girondes. Striking, plain, intense, student stuff. The vibrating edge of complementary colours. Viewers loved the immediacy. They were not very subtle, won no awards, but they sold well and paid the bills.

Wait, how did I get here?

My home country is very well run, so I never did social comment. There is little chance of catching the sight of tight-lipped royalty dressed in furs leaving the opera and ignoring open-mouthed beggars. I don't document people at work or at play. People pose, even when in a crowd; they collude in supposedly candid photographs. People are too complicated. What I wanted was the honest viewer.

Sliding. Slowing. Sliding.

I concentrated solely on the outside of the form to get to the inside of the viewer. I found the places that interested me, planned the shot, and came back prepared to impose myself on the scene. Anyone can take a realist photo with their phone. Few people, however, can take a picture of sand dunes and turn them into dark and light textured blocks of fabric that you want to reach out and touch.

Barn. Black. Isolated. Zoom out. Light surroundings. Papa gone. Call it Abandonment if you will. Is that an Adams or a White? Is that a Gironde?

You can destroy all my photos, all the prints, all the electronic images, the magazines, everything, but my ideas will still exist as objective knowledge. Whereas, if you destroy me, that is rather the end of it.

The ice cave was merely a temporary shell of ice hiding a death trap. We both could have died, but instead it will just be me. I knew that there is a hole behind me in the cave floor, which leads directly down - do not pass Go, do not collect four thousand krone - to the bottom of the glacier; in other words, I was sliding into a moulin, from which, rather like a black hole, no-one escapes.

Figures queued up on the edge of my awareness. They filed past my icy bed to say goodbye. Mama bent down to give me a kiss, and a fruit chew before I got on the taxi to school. Augustin punched me, gently, on the shoulder, and told me to get my guard up. Then he took up a newly printed photograph, the one of dark barns in the middle of nowhere. He nodded his head in agreement. He never said that he liked it.

Movement wasn't possible. I tried but it was like trying to wake up from a deep sleep. I was mentally alert but physically incapable. Anna – are you still watching that TV programme with the Hurtigruten ferry travelling up the coast? The boat should have reached Oksfjord by now. People want to get on TV so I am sure that there will be a crowd gathered at the wharf. I would have liked to go and see it, or even better, book a berth on the return journey to Bergen. Gliding over glass, over mirrors, moving through ripples, wiping the rain off the bow-cam. Helping the captain to put out a string of flags or pennants like bunting on the mast in front of the camera. We live in a beautiful country that is for sure. I hope I have contributed to the enjoyment of our surroundings.

It is a shame that I am stuck here, coat and clothes soaked in the narrow river of meltwater that will take me down the moulin. I am slipping away. You will be upset when you find out. I am sorry. Make sure you cry, yes, you must – you will need to let it all out. Remember Yvonne's funeral? You must howl. You must sob. Choke on the tears. Then tell a nice story about me.

It's OK, I am not in pain. I had an accident, a rather foolish accident. You will find out eventually, I hope.

The brush of a fly landing on my hand is like the brush of Gunnar's coat. Let's all go out for a walk together.

CHAPTER 17

T here was a boat moving on the lake, two people in the
wheelhouse, clear water parted by the bow, gulls following in the wake. The teenagers were shouting and playing.
Anna finished her lunch and watched the boat move along
the water, the connection between communities. Then a cry
went up, and a second yell, and then the calls were loud and
urgent, and the shouts of hilarity became cries for help.

She saw the first teenager, a boy with long black hair wearing a heavy metal T-shirt, slowly slide down from where he
was sitting on the rim of a bowl into an icy pool. He flailed
about trying to stop, but he continued down, gravity and the
icy lack of friction working against him. He slipped into the
freezing pool. The other boy, trying to help, bravely let himself fall after him. He ended up in the pool as well, holding onto his friend, who he tried to pull out, spluttering and
splashing to the edge. The boys struggled with one another
and began to sink lower under the water. The girls' shouts
for help grew louder as they panicked and tried to help the
drowning boys, without any grip on the ice, or the situation.

Anna crunched over the ice and reached the boys in the
pool. The struggling boy reached up for the walking stick she
offered but could not pull himself out.

'Hold on,' she said. 'Help is coming.' She stood back, tugging on the walking stick, but the boys weighed her down, and
all she managed was to hold them in the freezing water. Both
boys let go of the stick and grabbed for the edge of the pool.
Anna grabbed the youngest underneath the arms and tugged
as hard as she could. Slowly, she pulled the boy out of the pool
like a seal across the ice. She grabbed for the other boy in the
pool, but he was heavier, his skin shocked white, a blue line
around his lips. She also grabbed him under the arms, feeling
a weight that was too much for, and despite herself, grabbed
his hair and pulled him to the side of the pool.

'Sorry,' she told him, and she was scared to see the boy lose the life in his face and become even heavier. She had him up to the side of the pool, pushing his face up out of the water, trying to hold on.

'Call for help,' she told the hysterical girls. One of the girls pulled out her phone and looked at it. 'Call the rescue service,' she said, 'they'll come first.'

The boy fell slack in her arms, his face in the water. The rescue service would have to arrive instantly in their helicopter to do any good. 'Help me!' she yelled, and the youngest boy, shivering and dripping, got off the ice and grabbed his friend's arms. The girls tugged too, but they could not move him.

Not another death, she thought, she could not bear it. The girl was talking on the phone, giving their location. Anna had tilted the boy's head back so he could breathe. If not for her arms around his neck, he would have slipped away and drowned. The water rose over the edge of the pool, flooding the surface ice, soaking her where she lay, and making a foothold difficult. The boy's eyes were closed, his lips blue, his body slack.

'Hold on,' she whispered in his ear, 'we'll get you out,' and she heaved with all her might. The boy rose an inch further out of the pool, but he was too heavy to lift further. Anna and the girls pulled at his arms, at his hair, at his icy cold T-shirt, trying to haul him out of the water. 'Hold him steady,' she said, and she stood up ready to step in the pool; perhaps she could hang on to the side and push him out?

'No!' shouted a voice behind her. A young man, with a pointed blonde beard and short hair, wearing dark sunglasses, suddenly arrived by her side. He knelt by the edge of the pool, put his arms under the boy's shoulders and with a tremendous heave pulled him vertically out of the pool. He laid the boy prone on the ice. Anna looked at the badge on the newcomer's jacket. Twin jagged peaks: the guide had arrived at last.

The young man spoke to the boy and slapped his face. 'Can you hear me?' The boy lay still. The girls began to sob.

'What's his name?'

'Marco,' spluttered the other boy who was shivering, arms

wrapped around his body.

The guide sat Marco up and sat behind him, stripping him of his soaking shirt. 'Girls, give me your jackets.'

The girls obeyed, and the guide quickly wrapped the boy in the warm and dry jackets.

'Do you have hats?' said the guide. 'No, of course not. Help your friend. Sit with him, get him warm. Talk to him.'

Marco came slowly to life, gasping and flinching like a fish on the slab. He held one of the girls tight, and did not let go, as they tried to reassure him.

The guide called a number on his phone. Anna watched his eyes flash blue as he talked.

'Get his trousers off, wrap him up in anything warm.'

'I can't get them off,' the younger boy cried.

The guide reached down, a blade in his hand. He cut the boy's trousers away. 'Wrap him in your clothes, quickly. Wrap his body, then wrap his arms. Like this,' and he swaddled the boy, wrapping a shirt around his chest.

'Lift him up, get the jacket around him. Sit behind him and support his weight, talk to him, keep him happy.'

The guide's phone rang again, a melodic shrill. He spoke quickly, eyes fixed on Anna whom he now inspected. 'He needs attention in the medical centre,' he told her. 'People are coming to help.'

Two more people arrived, a man and a woman, both in their twenties she guessed, both dressed like the guide: carabineers, ice picks, sunglasses. The young woman skipped across the ice on her crampons like a young deer. When she reached the pool, she removed a silver thermal blanket from her backpack, and wrapped it around the boy.

The other guide, a solidly built man, bent down and lifted Marco, wrapped in an assortment of clothes like a vagabond, placing him over his shoulders, and carried him off the ice to where the boat waited on the lake.

The younger guide spoke to the children. The girls hugged one another and dropped their heads as the guide spoke. 'Glaciers are dangerous,' he told them, stamping his foot. 'They move, they surprise you.' Where's your guide? Where's your equipment? Your friend would have died if it wasn't for this woman.' He indicated Anna. 'Next time go with a guide. Now go with your friend.'

The children followed the young woman to the boat.

The guide turned to her. 'Are you Anna?'

She nodded, taking off her coat that was soaked where she had laid on the ice.

'I'm Lars.' He shook her hand. 'You saved the boy.'

'You did, really.' She checked that her jumper and leggings were dry.

Lars shook his head. 'You acted quickly. I saw you as I approached. Last year we lost a woman here, down a moulin, she slipped from up there,' he pointed up the glacier, 'and went all the way down. We heard her calling through the ice. We sent down a rope, but she was gone.'

Anna shook her head. 'People forget the danger.'

'Look,' said Lars. He pointed to a whirlpool on the edge of the lake. 'Her spirit is still here.'

Anna looked at the water and the currents moving in a circle. She was thinking about Emil, about such possibilities. On the first anniversary of Emil's disappearance, she had received a call from Rohde with some shocking news. The police had found a body, a male of similar age and build, badly decomposed, at a point well down the coast from Uektefjord, three kilometres away from where Emil was meant to be. She had travelled up with Birgit to identify the corpse. They had stopped at Oksfjord where the police had erected a white tent on the beach.

Birgit had held her hand as she entered the tent. Two forensic scientists were present dressed in blue overalls. The body lay covered on a trolley with wheels locked into position like a baby's pram. They were warned about the decomposition. When the cover was drawn back, it was a fairheaded man with a brown beard, shorter than Emil and ten years older. Outside the tent, she had remonstrated with the inspector.

Birgit had not been helpful or understanding. When they set about notifying Emil's side of the family of his disappearance, her sister had likened it to arranging a funeral, but without a body. We need a body; her sister had told her. Anna got the impression that any corpse would have done for her sister. Annoyed by her attitude, she took spiteful shots at the way Birgit dressed, the loose clothes she wore, the greying blonde hair she let frizz all over the place.

That had been the low spot, the nadir, her worst moment. But time passed, and there were no more calls to raise or ruin her hopes.

She watched the boat with the third guide and the children slide across the lake back to the village. She tried to imagine Emil swimming away to a better place.

'The boy will be fine,' Lars said. 'He'll think more clearly in the future.'

His companion, the female guide, came up to her. 'Hello, I'm Kristin.' She offered her hand. She was beautiful, slender, and tanned, with blonde hair under a black band.

'Anna, from near Burfjord.'

'You're going to Oksfjord?'

Anna shook her head. 'Uektefjord.'

Lars said: 'I've just come from there. It's an easy route. The glacial plateau is mostly flat. We have skis and rope for you so we can cross, but I see you have your own skis. If we find a crevasse, we need to stop and move around it.'

'And leave no litter, no yellow snow. I know the rules.'

'Do you need us, then? I see you have a map and a compass.'

'The ice shifts, the best route changes. And I'd appreciate the company.'

Kristin fiddled with the black Alice band that held her sunglasses on her pretty head. 'Are you going to Uektefjord to meet the guru, the giver of knowledge?'

'The guru again, that's twice today. I heard about him from a man called Tomas, who I met in the hut on the way.'

Lars' eyes lit up. 'Tomas, yes, I guided for him. He's an interesting man. Very well read. He knows everything.'

'This guru and his followers don't sound so bad, but anyway, I'm visiting family.'

Kristin looked at her. 'I was only joking. We've all heard about the tourists and their funny meetings outside. We had something similar in Finland for young people.'

Lars mumbled something, and Kristin knocked him on the

arm. 'We do appreciate nature, yes, our preacher likes to concentrate on that.'

'And when the evening comes...' said Lars.

Anna watched Kristin blush, was made aware of the lithe body unencumbered by children.

Kristin said, 'What I know of the guru at Uektefjord is that he doesn't preach, he doesn't tell people to do anything. If he says anything it is to suggest that people discover the desire in themselves to be good. That's what people are saying about him. You see, he wants people to prove themselves. It's not what you say but what you do that counts. He's a man of practical action.'

'Did you meet him?' Anna asked.

'Well, no, but it's what I've read about him, and what others have told me.'

'He doesn't sound like much of a threat, and not much help, either,' said Lars. In the distance, the boat rounded the corner of the lake and disappeared. 'What would be helpful is if children would stop coming up on the ice thinking they are Nansen.'

'You did the same when you were their age,' said Kristin. Lars shrugged.

'The young don't listen to anyone except themselves,' said Anna. 'Not until things go wrong.'

'And adults aren't much better,' said Lars. 'No matter how many rules we have on the ice, or off it.'

'We'd better get moving.' Kristin skipped away, as light as a foal, to fetch a spool of blue rope.

They walked up the glacier in a gentle ascent, the ice crunching beneath their feet. Anna felt herself get stronger as her view ahead expanded in all directions. The call of that boundless, silent space filled with ice was overwhelming. She felt the shackles of her life fall away as she strode out into infinity, leaving herself behind. Here, under the wide and boundless sky, she would have the freedom to think and let herself unravel.

CHAPTER 18

For a while there was only the crunch of crampons, on ice hundreds of feet thick below them. The retreat of the glacier was back through the original U-shaped valley it had created. Lars and Kristin showed Anna where the glacial arm had been last year, and now she saw bare rock smoothed of any plant life and polished boulders that suggested way-points.

The air was warm, and after an hour's walking Anna became hotter and slower with each step. She paused to drink water from her bottle, while Lars and Kristin waited patiently before they carried on. They passed many crevasses and manholes, the blues deepening the further down they peered. The ascent was only a mild gradient, but Anna was weary with each crunching trudge forward. The warmth, the exertion, the excitement of rescuing Marco, all had tired her out. Trudge, trudge, crunch, crunch, until she felt like a pack animal, a mule carrying supplies to remote hill farms. She looked up and saw the mountains ahead, and the icy tongue of the glacier widening into a snowy highway. Up on the plain, where they could ski, it would be easier. But now it was hard going.

Kristin walked behind her, as easy as a dancer, occasionally skipping forward to talk to Lars. Anna had never been that fit. Kristin reminded her of Nina, her niece, quick, clever Nina, who liked to dance. It was all about the flux of energy, she thought. The young take the energy from the old, and tire them out, but the old watch the young and it makes them feel young again.

Emil would have told her that all life comes from the sun, from its energy for photosynthesis in plants, to the animals that eat the plants, and the animals that eat the animals. A natural, healthy arrangement. Today the sun was too weak to dazzle, but it did ease her brow and soothe the pains in her knees.

Five metres ahead Lars stopped, and when Kristin and Anna caught up, they stood by his side. He pointed out an arête, a ridge between valleys. 'We go to the right. There's an observatory further on. It's an easy trip from then on.'

'Where's the observatory?' asked Anna.

'Beyond the start of the pass on the highest peak.' Kristin pointed northwards. The peaks were hidden in fog.

'We'd better move,' said Lars. His eyes locked with Anna's, and she was quite lost in their dazzling blue.

'How are you feeling? Kristin asked her.

'I'm not as fit as I was, but I'll be OK.' She spotted something on the ice and picked it up. 'What is this?'

'It's a geologist's hammer. My dad gave it to me,' said Kristin. She picked it up. 'Thank you, it must have slipped out of my pocket.' She turned it over in here hand. 'It's for tapping out fossils in rocks; they make good photographs. Lars, you carry it. I'm a klutz today.' Lars took the hammer with a smile.

She skipped back to her position behind Anna, who was even more aware of her age and Kristin's slender frame. She followed Lars as he walked ahead, trying to pick her feet up and match his long stride. A tortoise between two hares; it would be a very boring trip for them. After an hour's walk, as they climbed towards the plain, Lars called a halt, and they stopped for a water break.

Anna pointed into the distance. 'Is that our mountain?'

Lars glanced up. 'No, That's Haldde. We go up over Stortf-jell.'

'It looks like a long way away.'

'It's not that far to the observatory,' said Lars. 'Then we drop down into the valley and head for Uektefjord.' He helped Kristin back on with her rucksack. 'What have you got in there? It weighs a ton.'

'My make-up bag.'

'You don't wear make-up. You're pretty enough.' Lars ran his hand through Kristin's golden hair and let the strands fall between his fingers.

'You never know, I might meet a nice troll on the journey who needs charming.'

Lars looks at you, Kristin, as Emil looked at me, full of tenderness and love.

They moved on, stepping carefully over the ridges of ice piled up ahead. Each footfall was well placed and tested for solidity before stepping on. Once Lars' foot kicked open a pocket of air in the ice and the glacier yelped like a dog.

Anna, as the tortoise, took the last place in the race of three, and the two hares carried on their courting, Kristin prancing around Lars, who pretended not to notice. Anna stopped and peeled off her jacket and wrapped it around her waist. Lars and Kristin looked at her with dismay; the first rule of winter walking was to maintain several warm dry layers, and now their charge was behaving like a tourist rather than an experienced walker. They whispered amongst themselves.

'What did you say?'

'Your fleece will get wet if it rains. It's better if you keep your jacket over it.'

They were right, so she complied. 'Where are we?' she asked.

'Closing on Stortfjell,' Kristin said, pointing to a new peak now visible in the distance. 'In the middle is the virgin valley, Jomfrudalen.'

'Yes,' Lars said. 'Giant mountains and virgin valleys.'

'And reindeer too,' pointed Kristin. 'The Sami are nearby, driving the herds from the coast back into the interior. We will pass above them soon.'

They admired the animals, their long dark brown bodies, the elaborate ornamentation on their heads, antlers seemingly carved out of wood. A few reindeers straggled behind. And one, its wide black eyes shining like opals, came close enough for Lars to touch. Kristin's camera whirred. She beckoned Anna to join her and Lars in a shot with the reindeer behind them.

She showed the digital images to Anna. 'Have you noticed the shadows? They move sideways but not up and down. What a strange world.'

'You have a good eye,' she said. 'That's a nice camera.'

'From my father. I take photos for the university magazine.'

'A nice job as well.'

'It is,' said Kristin, 'the best job I've ever had. I love all this space. It helps you keep your head clear.'

'Even with Lars about?' smiled Anna.

'We're newly married,' she blushed.

'Where will you go after Uektefjord?'

'To Nordkapp. To see the puffin colony: over a million birds scattered over a hundred islands. We're going to have a look and get some pictures.'

'Oh, yes, the puffins. I heard about them on the radio,' she said. 'That's their breeding ground.'

'They last for the summer, and then they go back home,' said Kristin, 'but there's more than just puffins: geese and eagles too, skuas, cormorants. It's a fabulous sight. The birds fly in from many miles to make their nests.'

'Nature at its best.'

'Not quite,' said Kristin. 'There are crabs too, giant crabs.'

'How big are these crabs? When you say giant, how giant?'

'About this big,' and Kristin opened her arms. 'I was in Runde last year, in the south, during the breeding season: so many birds, thousands, hundreds of thousands of them. Gannets, beautiful birds, huge with wings as long as this,' she stretched her arms out wide. 'The kittiwakes are much smaller, and very funny. I took many photographs.' Kristin looked at Anna. 'What's Uektefjord like? Lars liked it but I've never been there.'

Anna knelt and fiddled with the laces of her crampons. 'It's a pretty place, as pretty as any along the north-western coast, but small enough for most ships to sail by, so it's not been spoilt. There's ice far out in the sea from the glacier, but it's oddly warm and pleasant. They say it has a white beach with sand.'

Anna walked on, with Kristin next to her. 'Who are you visiting?'

Anna's thoughts were at the coast, and then it was Birgit walking with her along the beach. 'My sister,' said Anna, and she tried to move people and houses in her mind so that her family were all together again.

CHAPTER 19

L ars upped the pace until the two women behind him were strung along the rope evenly. Stragglers in the reindeer herd were glimpsed below, striding to the lower ground for the winter. We three are typical of hard-headed humans, Anna thought, to move in the opposite direction, upwards into danger.

The sounds of animals barking surprised them all. They stopped still and listened.

'Dogs,' said Anna.

'Why are they barking?' asked Kristin.

'They've seen something they don't like.'

'Maybe the reindeer?'

'Maybe, but reindeer and dogs are used to one another.'

They stood still for a few more moments, and Anna noticed how the barking had served to bond their own little pack together. After a while, they heard nothing more.

Lars brought out his ice axe and prodded the ice ahead of him. 'We'll ski from here. The snow is good.'

Anna sat down and took off her crampons, wrapping the metal shoes in a piece of leather in her rucksack. She took out her ski boots, wrapped in a plastic bag, smelling of a new layer of wax. With an extra pair of socks on, her feet fitted well in the ski boots, and she did up the bindings. It had been a while since she had skied cross-country, but the broad boots and skis fitted as snugly as ever. She tied her walking stick to her rucksack and picked up her ski poles, which came up to her shoulders, and when she finally had her gloves on, she felt ready to go.

When she looked up, she was struck by a sight. Lars and Kristin stood a few metres apart in the same pose, with their backs to her, looking at the way ahead. Each held their ski poles ready one in each hand and placed on the ice. They were smartly dressed, no loose clothing, everything was tucked in, they had hats and sunglasses, and shone as they stood under the bright azure sky. Their poses said that they were ready for action, whereas Anna was ready for a rest.

She glided up to them. They smiled, touched gloved hands together, and set off. Lars was soon ahead with Kristin behind. Anna did her best to keep up, as the familiar cadence of skiing came back to her over the sparkling glacier. Ahead were a few man-high rocks littered across a flat plain, otherwise the way ahead looked easy. There was no better place to be than here, under the blue sky, with the world so easy to move over.

An hour later the terrain had changed to uneven snow that looked like mud or salt flats. Her heart was pounding from the exercise, a sheen of sweat on her forehead, while Lars and Kristin looked cool and fresh. The rocks were now hills painted black, brown, and white. Snow clouds filled the sky. For a while life looked rosy; and then she was reminded of where and who she was. Kristin was next to her unspooling a blue rope.

'8 mil?' asked Anna?

'Ten.' Kristin looped coils of the rope over her shoulder and Anna did the same.

'I remember.' She wound the rope around her shoulder and tied off the loops, clipping the remainder in a karabiner. Lars tied himself on, and they spread out, so that he was the in middle, with Kristin first and Anna behind him.

'You are the client,' smiled Lars. 'We will go into any crevasse before you.'

'You mean I will, dear husband.'

'You are light, I will pull you out.'

Lars tested the rope between them. 'Hold it like this,' he told Anna, 'with one hand only. Keep about ten metres apart.'

Kristin did up Anna's jacket to the top of her neck. 'Have you got a hat?'

Anna looked at her. 'There's a hood on the jacket, but I like it down.'

Kristin pulled the hood up; it did not fit very well. 'Have this,' she said, and Kristin put her woollen hat on Anna's head. Anna felt like a child being dressed by its teacher or parent.

'It's not far on the glacier, and we'll be able to stop at the observatory for a rest,' said Lars. 'Pull on the rope if you see any crevasses, although we should see them first. Are we ready?'

'Yes, my love,' said Kristin.

'Last one to the observatory is a troll,' said Anna.

With the rope held lightly between them, they resumed skiing across the glacier, the blue rope drooping between them. Anna breathed in the sweet cool air and listened to the meltwater recede. The glacier appeared lighter and the mountains darker, their progress over the ice as smooth and as quiet as sleep. They slid over the plain, which expanded and retreated away to the horizon, the mountain tops looking down on them.

Beauty, clarity, peace and humility, these are the things nature gives me, thought Anna, as she skied along. She felt the muscles in her shoulders unknot and relax. She imagined her woes beginning to deposit on the ice, like the black soot of animal debris. She was being cleansed by the ice and sun, soothed of her anxieties by the hiss of her skis.

She had never found glaciers to be bleak, unlike Fridtjof who regarded the immensity of snow and ice as a hostile place. Perhaps Fridtjof didn't like how there was so much empty space which could not be controlled: the manholes, the caves, the hidden depths. This was a difficult place, yes, but it was not harsh or evil, merely indifferent. Take one path and survive. Take the other and fall to your death; the ice couldn't care less about you.

They skied past white hummocks, which reminded Anna of snow-covered bodies, Gunnar in his grave who might be hidden now, a thought she found comforting. A roar in the distance halted their tiny column. Two sheets of ice collided together, and a new range of peaks rose into the sky. The new summits were topped by an ever-changing show of colours as the light refracted through the changing angles. The ice growled and roared but the glacier did not flinch and neither did she.

She suspected that Fridtjof did not like the message of the ice, and of those that were happy to explore it. Fridtjof liked his orchards and his soft fruits, Siegfried's boat on the placid fjord, Alva's European cooking. He was proud to be the warden at the village church, and to be a parent governor at his children's school. Fridtjof would not see the point in Nansen or any other of the polar explorers' quest for the poles; they were quests for nothing, imaginary signs in the ground, places reachable in theory but which moved with the turning of the Earth and the passing of time.

'Listen,' said Lars, and they listened. 'Water.' He pointed to rivulets on the ice. 'That means we are near the crevasse zone. There will be wet snow hiding the crevasses, keep alert.'

They moved on, keeping the regulation spacing between them, Kristin leading the way. They went forward a hundred metres, then Lars stopped again. The landscape had changed ahead.

The army could not have done a better job in creating an obstacle to stop movement across the land. The ice rose at multiple ridges, each shard twenty or thirty feet high, each one at a steep angle. Skis were hung off rucksacks, crampons were tied onto ski boots.

Kristin showed Anna how to tackle the challenge. Plant the ice axe into the wall of ice, climb up the slope, find footholds with the crampons, put your weight forward on gloved hands, and then, without losing balance, pull out the ice axe and repeat.

Anna found it to be exhausting work, whereas for Lars and Kristin it seemed to be a form of mild exercise. They waited patiently, watching Anna climb to the top of a ridge, and then walk down unsteadily to the bottom of another ridge, only to repeat the challenge over another wall. It was like an assault course. Lars claimed that it was the shortest way through the crevasses, and if that were true, it was not a quick route. She climbed up another ridge, balanced on top, walked down the side, and saw that there were still multiple obstacles to climb over. She felt the sweat soaking her shirt, the surest way to lose heat. And to think she could have taken a boat up the coast to Uektefjord if she hadn't decided to up sticks and run away.

But this was the challenge she had chosen. Emil, or some evidence of him, might be lying in a crevasse. Inspector Rohde had flown his helicopters over the glacier, with infrared cameras, but he didn't have the inclination to do it again. She looked at the challenge ahead. There was no other way across a route that aimed for the high, navigation points. Otherwise, they could have gone for the lower routes, around the edge of the glacier, through seemingly impenetrable forests.

'There's a big one ahead,' said Lars.

More than a crevasse, it was an icy stream ten feet wide. The snow was melting around it, revealing in places scrub underneath. The rocks were slippery with wet snow. Lars walked along the side of the crevasse one way, and Kristin walked in the opposite direction. When they came back, they agreed that the crevasse was too wide to step over.

He took a pole and sunk it in the stream up to the handle. In this manner he tested the depth and stability of the watery crevasse. In one place the pole went in only halfway up. Kristin tested another pole in a nearby spot with the same result.

Lars was laughing. 'Are you ready, Nansen? We need to jump this one. Give me your skis'. Anna handed hers over, as did Kristin. Lars tied all three pairs to his rucksack and put the pack on.

'I will go first.' Kristin steadied herself at the edge of the stream, tramping down the snow until the scrub showed through with no further holes. Then she took a couple of steps back, moved forward and skipped over the stream in one fluid motion. She stood on the other side, waiting until she was certain she was on solid ground. 'Your turn, dear husband.'

'Thank you, darling wife.'

These two are as Emil and I were all those years ago. Nothing was too much trouble back then, and if we did meet an obstacle, we went over it together.

Lars stood ready. He was loaded like a mountain porter with his rucksack and three pairs of tall skis poking out the top. He walked forward, planted both poles in the middle of the stream, and strode across the stream as if it was solid ground. 'Bravo,' said Kristin. They both turned and looked at her. 'Your turn, Anna. Do you want the poles?'

A shining, flowing obstacle stands in my way; yet another barrier in my hopeless quest. She took off her rucksack and threw it across the stream to Kristin. Lars took off his sunglasses to see her better. 'Please, don't look. If you hear a splash, then you may pull me out.' To her surprise they both turned around and looked the other way. She imagined the back of Lars to be the back of Emil. The stream disappeared as she ran up and stepped out into space. Her leading boot hit the edge of the stream and Kristin pulled her over.

Lars bowed his head. 'Very good, Nansen. Your long legs give you an advantage.'

They were vigilant for running surface water, and found more crevasses, but none as wide as the first. Soon the way ahead was navigable again on skis. They followed Lars, sliding in his tracks, three figures with the rope slack between them on the ice. The side of the mountains framed their way ahead, down a walled tunnel, along a white road. The way expanded as they moved onto the widest part of the glacier, and the horizon receded into the whiteness under the blue sky.

This is the point of my journey, Anna thought, where the mind can become clear, and one can stand as a speck in the middle of the universe.

The wind blew up and filled the air with snow and the noise of rushing trains. Her skis hit hidden rocks, and she fell over. The rope tightened and she felt it tug Kristin ahead, but her guides were lost in the sudden storm.

Anna was on the ground, snow stuck to her jacket and trousers and frozen in patches. She looked at the white powder and inspected it on her gloves. The rope had come untied from her karabiner. The wind suddenly strengthened and made it difficult to move forward. She leant against the wind and imagined pushing against a strong man with ice in his beard.

Boreas teased her, making her put all her weight on one leg, then changing tack to buffet the other side of her body. She dragged her left leg forward with the ski sticking out awkwardly to the side. Her poles were in the ground and should have given support, but it was more as if she was stuck between them and was being pulled apart. She pushed into the wind, and the wind pushed back. She persevered as if she were dragging an enormous weight. Boreas, you will need to do better than that, for I am a stubborn mule.

The wind dropped. She was in a sea of white, with the black-topped rocks running towards her like waves. The worse thing was that, behind her, the sun lit the sky in a beautiful silvered backdrop with a few scudding clouds. It would be so easy to just turn around and give up, citing the weather as too difficult, but they must be closer to Uektefjord than home.

With another heave she pulled her left leg forward, waited, panting, and then trudged on raising her right ski. She pushed down on her poles and moved a little ahead. The upward slope was now against her. She was tired. Her foot hurt. She was an embarrassment. Her guides must have thought she wanted to come out here to die. Suicide by misadventure. She would not be the first person to do it in the winter when the sky turned dark all day.

Kristin appeared with her face covered in a scarf and reattached the rope to Anna's karabiner. 'You are wheezing.'

'Asthma, made worse by the cold.'

'You should have said.' Kristin yanked on her rope and Lars joined them.

'I didn't want to slow you down.' She wished she were back at the summer farm, or in Inari with Birgit and the girls. They would go out on the lake to catch some fish for supper. In the evening, they would watch movies together in a warm room with a fire. Instead, she had opted to torture herself like a medieval pilgrim. She was no trekker, and her destination was pulled out of a hat. Kristin and Lars talked together quietly, occasionally looking at her. But she had to go on, for Emil, for herself. She had to push past Boreas and get on with the rest of her life, the tightness in her chest be damned.

Lars finished his inspection of the sky and the route ahead. 'This is definitely the last day trek of the season. But we will get to Uektefjord tomorrow morning, unless we can catch reindeers and fly.'

Anna sighed. 'Like Peer Gynt over the mountain, into the

halls of the mountain king.'

Kristin came over and did up Anna's jacket to the neck. 'You go in the middle and follow Lars.' Kristin kissed her cheek. 'You're stronger than you think; you just need to keep going.'

I'm not strong; I'm tired out, and exhausted from trying so hard. It would be nice if things could be a bit easier for me. But she didn't say the words and took her place in the middle of the line as they set off under the twilight sky.

CHAPTER 20

The frustration in Lars' voice was obvious. He had moved Anna to the front so that she could set the pace. He seemed fed up having to wait for her, even though he was the guide, receiving a fee for his work, she thought. Then they told her that they had no tent, because they had not expected the crossing to take so long.

Anna strode ahead for a while, hoping to put on a good performance, like a willing dog pulling a sled, trying always to please its master. But whenever she looked behind, her guides were right behind her, Lars looking especially grim. The ice became less firm and was replaced by snowdrifts into which Anna sank with each footfall. She stumbled on, with Kristin, then Lars, propping her up on either side. When Anna lost her footing a final time, she sank to her knees in the snow and didn't get up.

'Let's have a break,' said Kristin. 'We will ski from here.'

'You're not even sweating,' Anna took off her hat and wiped the icy sheen from her face.

'I'm fit; I walk in the country a lot.' Kristin broke out her a bar of chocolate and shared it round. 'How are you feeling?'

'My lungs are on fire. The insides of my thighs and the backs of my legs are sore and stiff.' She munched on the chocolate. 'How far to the observatory?'

Lars grunted. 'At this rate, about a week.'

'Am I really that slow? I thought we were doing well.'

'It's early evening. Off the glacier, down the valley to Uektefjord is another six hours easily.'

'So, we will arrive in the early hours, in the moonlight.'

'We'll probably make it,' said Lars. 'The weather is fair, but we can go no slower.'

Anna kicked Lars in the shin with her boot. She liked to see the surprise on his face. 'Of course, you must goad the mule to make sure she makes the journey,' said Anna. 'I understand. I apologise for holding us back, but I'm sure I'm doing alright.'

A smiled slowly appeared on Lars' face. 'That's the spirit, Nansen.' He took his compass out and looked around at the peaks. Then they heard a sound carried to them on the wind. A howl that rose and fell in pitch and ended on a long mournful note.

Lars was amazed. 'It's a wolf!'

Anna listened again to the singing howl. 'A lonely wolf.'

Kristin looked about. 'Where is it?'

'Somewhere behind us.' Lars took out his binoculars and scanned the way they had come. Another howl reached them, another song, rising and falling.

'I can't see any wolves on the ice,' said Lars. 'They must be up on the rocks.' He swung his binoculars up and searched the mountainside. He spotted the animal when it called again, head raised up out of the cover of the rocks and silhouetted against the sky: the intelligent face, the dark almost black fur, the long nose, and open jaws.

Beside Lars, a digital shutter clicked as Kristin captured the scene.

Anna took the camera from Kristin, focused on the animal, and zoomed in on its head. It barked again, and she saw the flash of its teeth. 'It really is a wolf,' she said. Then the animal turned towards her, and she took a shot of its attractive head and short ears.

All three of them were excited to see a second wolf appear and stand next to the first: light legs, dark grey coat, light snout, ears out wide.

'They're a mating pair,' Anna breathed.

'She's after the sun and he's after the moon,' said Kristin.

'Are they a pair?' asked Lars. 'How can you tell?'

Anna just shrugged. 'I know animals, especially dogs, and wolves are not so different.'

Lars exhaled a breath of misty air. 'This is incredible; there are hardly any wolves about. Just a few families. Wolves in this country are nearly extinct.'

Anna continued to watch through the camera. 'They're fighting for their survival.'

'They are protected,' said Lars. 'It's illegal to kill them.'

'Something's gone wrong. They're up here perhaps because

they're already being hunted, driven away from the sheep or reindeer. What else will they eat?'

'As long as it's not us, that's fine,' said Kristin. 'I've only seen a wolf once before, prowling around a hut on a previous walk. It came out of the darkness one evening and gave me a real scare.'

'We'll be fine. There's nothing for them on the ice.'

'Will wolves follow us across the ice?' asked Kristin.

Anna looked at her. 'We train huskies and dogs to go on the ice. For wolves it would be no problem.' She remembered when a wolf had appeared at the summer farm; it had come up to the door and looked in the window. Gunnar had jumped up onto the sofa, and stood nose to the glass barking at it, the two animals separated by a thick sheet of glass. In the end, the wolf went away.

'Can you call your friends, the other guides? See if anyone has seen the wolves?' Anna asked Lars.

'OK,' shrugged Lars. He called a number on his mobile, turning his back into the wind so he could hear the person on the other end.

Anna watched him nodding as he spoke. 'Anything?' she said when he had finished.

'I've reported it, but no one has seen anything. There will be a fuss now, I think. Wolves are protected.'

'What about tourists? They'll get a shock,' said Kristin.

'There are no hires out for long trips. Only tourists standing on the arms of the glacier this morning. They will have gone back to their hotels by now.' Lars shook his head. 'This is a crazy place for a holiday. Tourists go to Tromsø, Nordkapp, Hammerfest, or Alta. No one goes over the glacier the whole way. We usually take hires up for two hours on the glacier at a time, then we come back.'

'Maybe some of the tourists have the northern spirit. They appreciate the beauty of nature, the simplicity, they like to be alone with their thoughts.'

'It is beautiful up here, that's for certain,' said Lars. 'And I do love this job.' He cupped Kristin's face in his hand, 'And I love you,' he whispered, 'you are elfin fair.'

Kristin blushed and looked away. 'Not the old words,' she

whispered.

'But beauty fades,' said Lars, turning away. 'Once you've been out on the ice for a few days, sleeping in a freezing tent, you get very tired of eating boiled reindeer meat and any roots you can dig out of the ground with your axe, or drinking melted snow.'

'It sounds exciting at first,' agreed Kristin, 'but in the end we need companions, consolation, civilisation.'

'I know,' said Anna. 'It becomes more about survival than actually enjoying life.'

Kristin frowned. 'I've been thinking about this guru character, Ritz. He lands in Uektefjord, builds a hotel, and tells everyone it is a utopia. He has a good sense of humour!'

'Tomas said it was a beautiful villa. People sit around and discuss things like how to be good and kind to people. I've no idea what else they do.'

'Not trekking, I bet,' said Lars.

'It sounds like university,' said Kristin. 'We used to sit and discuss politics, the state of the world, Norway's problems, the oil and fishing. Then we always got onto religion. There were people with strong views and some people with none who just listened. It may be something like that.'

'Maybe there will be some weirdos, you know, like in a cult; naked ceremonies under the midnight sun.' Lars stroked his beard to a point and his eyes gleamed with the idea.

'You wish, Lars.'

He laughed. 'The snow and ice changes people. It makes them do crazy things.'

'I think all you have to do is think of the other person,' said Anna. 'That's what we ask of the children at school.'

'That's not always easy to do,' said Kristin,

'It seems to be the hardest thing in the world sometimes. But I tell you what I really hope there is at the end.'

'What?'

'Chocolate cake - I'm starving!'

'Not for me,' said Kristin holding her belly. 'I don't feel too good, my stomach is doing flip-flops.'

'Come on,' said Lars, 'we must get on, time is passing. It's getting cold, and we have no good furs to keep us warm.'

Anna did up her jacket and pulled her hat over her ears. It was indeed much colder. The wind searched inside her jacket, looking for where she lived. And now the wind had a sound, a permanent howl in the background.

Lars was listening to the wind. 'Boreas breathes like that when he's ready to make a storm. You know about Boreas?'

Anna nodded. 'I've met him.'

'You and your stories,' said Kristin. 'We'll reach the observatory and then we'll be in a sheltered valley all the way down to Uektefjord.'

'At least the wolves have gone,' said Anna.

They put on their skis. Lars checked the rope which ran between the carabineers on their belts. 'Follow me, no craziness.'

They set off again on solid snow, using their poles to push up a gentle slope on skis, heading into a growing expanse of white. Nature's palate was drab and lit by the sun on the horizon. Along the way, Anna felt her muscles ache and stiffen further; she wondered just how energetic she would be in the face of adversity. Words were easy, actions were difficult. The black mountains ahead looked no fun at all. They headed right off an arête towards the valley that would take them to the coast.

Boreas now howled persistently around them. She hoped that the observatory was not much further. Lars had explained their position, and how he had reckoned magnetic north, while telling her, like a knowledgeable child, about the three North poles, and their definition, and then about how the Earth rotated on its axis, and why she could expect one morning to wake up with the moon on her face.

She just wanted to get to Uektefjord by any means possible.

CHAPTER 21

Siegfried uncovered Gunnar's body one stone at a time. He wore black rubber gloves and placed the white stones to one side of the grave.

Fridtjof prodded the body with a stick broken from a tree. Grey ash blew up in the air as he poked about. 'She used lime.' He unocvered some haf-burnt black bricks in the grave 'And some charcoal to burn the body. The rain put out the fire soon enough.'

Fridtjof had his scarf wrapped over his mouth and sounded muffled and unhappy. 'Why did she do this? This is a poor effort at burial. This is a scandal. We must not mention this to anyone. Anna has not been right since Emil went missing, but she is too stubborn to take any help.'

'Perhaps she did not like the smell?' said Siegfried. He removed more stones and uncovered the hindquarters. 'Also, Gunnar was a large dog. She would have had to dig a deep grave.'

Both men stepped away as the smell of decomposition swirled in the air holding scarves to their faces. 'I will dig a proper grave here with Steinar's help. He is young and fit and he will make the grave deep.'

Fritdjof turned his gaze to the church by the edge of the fjord. 'We should honour Emil as well.'

'What if Anna finds Emil on her travels?'

'That is very unlikely.'

Siegfried picked up the pot of red geraniums and placed it on the wall bordering the pasture. He lit a cigarette and the end turned red as he inhaled.

'Anna needs help in her situation.' Fridtof accepted another cigarette lit by Siegfried and drew in the smoke.

'What help could we give her?' Siegfried rested against the wall, enjoying his smoke. 'If Alva were to disappear, what help could I give you? Or if my Greta vanished, what could you do for me?'

'You would search for her with me, old friend, wouldn't you?'

'Of course, as we all searched for Emil. We were out for days on the glacier, and all along the coast, and all points in between, and we found nothing. We went home empty-handed.' Siegfried coughed and put a hand on his chest. 'Poor Anna has had to live without Emil for a long time, yet the pain is still raw.' He stared at the shallow grave. 'At least Gunnar was there to keep her company.'

The two men were silent for a while. Siegfried stepped over the wall and inspected the sheep cairn. White bones peeked up through a gap in the dark stones. Fridtjof joined him. 'She was in two minds, I think. Torn between burying Gunnar as one would a person, or disposing of him as an animal, as quickly as possible.'

They stood back over the grave and Siegfried noticed the burnt fabric under Gunnar's body. 'She wrapped him in his blanket. That was a loving touch.'

Fridtjof snorted. He looked around the farm and up into the hills. 'This is a woman who cared so much she had to run away?'

'Put yourself in her shoes, dear friend.' Siegfried did up his jacket as the wind began to bite. 'First Emil, then Gunnar. This is the place where her life soured like leftover milk. She lost her husband, and then she lost her dog. Which one of us would want to stay with those ghosts hanging around?' Siegfried stubbed his cigarette into the ground. 'Come on, I have the tractor, I will take you home.'

The men walked back to the farmhouse, and the tractor waiting by the barn. Silje and her flock were huddled under the trees nearest to the farmhouse.

'Steinar can also take the flock down to my orchards,' said Fridtjof.

Siegfried looked around the summer farm. 'We should persuade Anna to do something with this place. Either renovate it for the winter, or lease it out, or sell it. She cannot manage it alone in the winter, not in this state. She should stay with her sister in Inari.'

The two men stopped outside the barn. 'That was messy

work,' said Siegfried. 'Let's have a drink, to wash away the smell of death.' He pulled upon the barn doors, and they entered, walking past more tractors and farming equipment. The loft area was reached by a set of wooden stairs at the back of the building. The steps were made from rough planks that promised to leave splinters in their hands as they made their way up. Both men bowed their heads ducking through the narrow gap at the top of the stairs

They emerged onto a wide wooden platform covered with hundreds of red potatoes scattered throughout a bedding of straw. The faint smell of fermentation was present, a pleasant winey smell. Along one side of the wall was a copper vessel and a still on a bench above which was a cupboard.

Siegfried lifted the lid off a stainless-steel vessel and inhaled the aroma. He inspected the twelve-volt battery on the floor. The wires ran up to a flat black hot plate.

'Is the new arrangement working well?' asked Fridtjof.

'Very well.' Siegfried. 'The hot plate is much safer than a naked flame.' His hand ran along the coiled pipe they called the worm.

'That is the way we started with Varg.' Fridtjof crossed himself.

Siegfried completed his inspection of the apparatus. 'Some of the old ways carry on. This set-up will last a good while.' He took two mugs off hooks on the wall.

Fridtjof settled down on a wooden chair to look out through a small door with a window at the end of the loft area. There was a pulley from which a thick rope hung down to the ground below. 'Steinar can do the heavy lifting this season. Pull the potatoes up in a bucket.' He laughed. 'We must make sure we do not wear the young man out.'

Siegfried poured a generous splash of a clear liquid into a chipped and enamelled mug. 'With coffee or apple juice?'

'Apple. I've had my coffee for the day. Anymore and I'll be leaving Alva the farm'.

'What did the doctor say?'

'Some exercise, some alcohol, but less coffee.' Fridtjof shook his head.

Siegfried handed him the mug. Fridtjof waited for him to

pour his own drink, tempered with coffee. 'It's always karsk for you.'

'I have a snow plough to drive. I need to stay sharp.'

They chinked mugs. 'To faithful Gunnar.'

'And to the unfortunate Emil.'

They were silent a while.

'To brave Anna.' They chinked mugs again.

Fridtjof swirled his drink around in the mug. 'Does she really think Emil is out there, frozen in the ice?'

Siegfried shrugged. 'I once found a man in the snow who had been out drinking. He had fallen off his bike into a drift and couldn't get out. He survived because of the cold the doctors told me.' Siegfrid clinked his mug again with Fridtjof's. 'Skal!' they declared together.

There was a noise outside of someone walking up the stony path. Fridtjof looked out of the window. 'It is Tuva, Steinar's wife. She is heading towards the milking shed. Brunost and prim for the weeks ahead.'

Both men stood up slowly, holding their backs.

'Ready to clear the way in your plough?'

'As long as there is no-one hidden in a drift.'

They descended the stairs carefully and shut up the barn.

CHAPTER 22

S ome way along their route, stood a vertical wall of ice and snow.

'An avalanche,' said Lars. He pointed upwards. 'Look, from that overhang.'

They peered up towards where the ice had split off a huge overhanging cliff and fallen down the mountain side. There were trees all around, knocked over and uprooted like weeds.

'We're lucky this fell before we got here,' said Lars. 'Or we would have been in trouble.'

'It's immense,' said Anna, 'like a castle wall.' Her gloves slipped up and down the sheer icy face. 'How do we go around? Is this the end?' She felt herself ready to break like glass.

'It's not the end,' said Lars. 'I've climbed over bigger obstacles.' He looked at Anna 'Do you like books?'

She nodded.

'Do you always read a book to the end? Or do you give up halfway if you're not enjoying it.'

Anna patted the wall of snow and ice. 'Always to the end, no matter how drawn out or difficult.'

Lars was smiling. 'And how do you manage that?'

'One chapter at a time, sometimes only one page, until the going gets easier. If we give up as teachers, then how can we expect the children to keep going?' She looked up to the top of the wall. Another obstacle on my trek, to be taken one step at a time. Another delay to finding out what happened to Emil, and if there is nothing to be found, so be it.

'We will use the ropes and axes,' said Lars. 'I'll go first and haul us up.'

Anna looked at Kristin. 'I'm not a size nine, you know. Lars won't be able to lift me into the sky like a crane.'

'I will use my super strength,' said Lars. He opened Kristin's rucksack, took out a rope, and put on a purple helmet. He tapped the hard hat. 'It will keep my brains in if I fall.'

'You haven't got any brains,' said Anna. 'Now you think you're Superman, trying to climb up there.'

'Such a lack of faith in her fellow man,' Lars said to Kristin.

'I've got faith in things that are possible, not things that are not.'

'That's not faith, then,' said Lars.

'Good luck,' said Kristin, and she kissed him on the cheek. 'No showing off.'

'I'll go first, then it will be your turn. Kristin will help you get a grip on the ice. You will climb and I will pull, and you will come up the wall.'

Lars clanged the metal crampons on his boots together. He stood next to the ice wall, reached up and thrust an axe in the ice above his head. He kicked the toe of his boot into the ice and the crampon held. With one leg up, he kicked the other boot into the ice, and stood, half crouched. He struck his other axe into the ice face. Then he moved his feet and repeated the cycle of stepping up and placing his axes over his head.

'He's doing it,' said Anna.

'Of course,' said Kristin, 'he's strong.'

Lars moved steadily up the face of the ice wall, axes sinking into the ice, boots kicking new footholds. At the top he doubled up over the wall and disappeared.

'I can't do that,' said Anna. 'He's obviously an expert but look at me; I'm not so fit.'

'Lars will have you on a rope. You need faith in yourself,' said Kristin. 'Why not believe it can happen?'

Anna looked up into the bright sky and to the top of the ice wall far above her. 'I'm scared. Is there no other way?'

'Look around. We're in a steep valley sealed by a wall. We need to climb out. Walking round will take for ever and we might lose the route.'

Lars appeared at the top of the wall and called down. 'It's clear from here all the way to the coast.'

'He's just saying that to cheer me up, isn't he?' said Anna. 'We're still in the valley; how can he see the coast?'

'Anna, what choice do we have? We're on this trek. You are on the journey of a lifetime. There's no going back.'

Lars threw down the rope. 'Heads!' he called. The purple helmet fell into the snow. Anna put on the helmet, which wobbled around on her head. Kristin helped Anna into the harness. 'He's a climber, always insists on being prepared.' She tied the rope onto Anna's waist karabiner and through the harness.

'I'm like a worm on a hook,' said Anna.

'You are funny,' smiled Kristin. She called up to Lars and repeated what Anna had said.

Lars shook with laughter and mimed casting a fishing line down the cliff.

'He's a strong fisherman,' said Kristin, 'but you will need to walk up.' She led Anna to the ice wall. 'Stand here,' she said. 'First we get a toe hold. Kick here and stand up.'

Anna kicked at the wall. A small sliver of ice fell off. The ice axe appeared in her hand.

'Throw the axe in hard!' shouted Kristin. 'You want to climb this wall. You will climb this wall!'

Anna struck the axe in the wall and kicked with the toe of her boot at the wall.

'Go on, step up and stay still.'

Anna put her weight on the right foothold and hung suspended on the ice wall.

'Use the other foot. Lars will keep the rope tight. You won't fall.'

Anna plunged the axe in again, kicked her left boot at the wall, and held steady. She pressed her body against the ice, cold cheek against frozen wall.

Lars shouted something to Kristin from on high.

'He says you're heavy.'

'I did mention it,' she wheezed.

'Now, you make new handholds and footholds, and up you go.'

Anna kicked again into the wall and her boots held, balanced on the toes of the crampons. The strength was failing in her arm, but she managed to get the top of the axe in the ice wall. The rope moved up and Lars hoisted her skywards, her jacket bunching up under her shoulders.

'Excellent!' cried Kristin. 'You're doing well!'

'I'm too tired!' called Anna. 'I can't do this.'

Kristin called up to Lars in a language Anna did not understand. The rope tightened and Anna found herself kicking at the ice wall and moving upwards. The ice axe fell from her hand. Lars stood with the rope wrapped around his waist and running through his giant hands; pulling hand over hand he brought Anna ever closer. At points in her journey she had the merest touch on the wall. She cried out in pain as the rope cut through her jacket and jumper under her arms. And then she reached the top of the ice wall and Lars dragged her over. She lay on her belly at the top in the refreshing breeze. A vast plain of ice lay ahead of her.

She felt Lars' hands all over, rolling her over sideways, undoing the rope, retrieving the harness. 'That hurt, Nansen.' Through shredded gloves she saw that his hands bore red lines on the palms. Anna rolled over on to her back, and saw him sat atop the wall, legs over the edge, with the rope tied to Kristin, wound around his middle as if he were a thick tree. Kristin appeared at the top of the wall, walking over the lip with the ice axe in hand. 'You have a lovely technique,' said Lars. Kristin gave him a kick, then saw the state of his hands, and gave a little cry.

Anna looked over the top of the avalanche at the height she had scaled. The valley proceeded towards a dim grey horizon. Kristin was smiling at her, offering a chocolate bar, which she accepted. Lars was pacing about, smearing his hands with a tube of white cream pulled from his rucksack, the pain intermittent on his face.

'I'm sorry,' she told Lars.

'For what, for having mass?' He laughed. 'That would be a sorry thing.'

Kristin tended to Lars, bandaging his hands. Anna surveyed the route ahead. Snow stuck to her face. It was a white world now; when she had left it had been a world of green and blues, red and yellows. This was a world of black and white, a stripped-down world, where mass and necessity collided like billiard balls. She listened to the growing wind and watched the snow swirl in dense clouds around them.

CHAPTER 23

S iegfried arrived with Steinar to dig Gunnar's grave. As the two men stepped out of the tractor, Steinar put out his hand to feel the first flakes of falling snow.

'We need to be quick,' said Siegfried. They lifted Gunnar's corpse away from the grave, faces turned away from the smell and the evidence of animals' investigation. Steinar took a shovel and started to dig in the shallow bowl Anna had made.

Siegfried removed a wooden coffin from off the back of the tractor.

'How special was this dog to get a coffin?'

'He was an ordinary dog,' said Siegfried, 'but a faithful companion to an extraordinary woman. Anna never gave up hope of seeing Emil again, although it surely cost her a piece of her mind.' He laid the coffin flat on the ground. The coffin was plain wood, made, and donated by the Olsen shipyard.

'Mrs Nordstrom taught me at school when I was an infant. Tuva remembers her as well.' Steinar returned to his work piling dark soil in a mound by the side of the grave. 'She was a good teacher and a kind woman.' Steinar continued his work he could stand in the grave up to his waist. From a spot in the pasture near the sheep cairn, he cut several neat pieces of turf and stacked them next to the side of the grave. 'I have never dug such a deep grave for a dog.'

'Gunnar was a big dog.' Siegfried looked towards the church on the edge of the fjord. 'Fritdjof wanted to start a plot in the churchyard for the Nordstroms. A memorial for Emil, then a grave for Gunnar, would you believe it, and a plot reserved for Anna.' He laughed. 'Sometimes he gets ahead of himself.'

'He thinks he is the pastor.' Steinar lit a cigarette and drew in the smoke. When he had finished, he stubbed the butt on the edge of his shovel and tossed it into the grave. Siegfried gave him a look and he fished it out again. 'I hope people bother so much about me when I go.'

'You are much too young to worry about such a thing. I will be ready long before you.' Siegfried lowered his voice. 'Make sure that they serve everyone a cup of my hjemmebrent, with coffee or apple, as they wish.'

Steinar laughed. 'Fridtjof would have a fit.'

'I think you will find him amenable.' Siegfried looked at Gunnar's body. 'Time to be strong and hold our breath.'

Together they lifted Gunnar's body into the coffin and closed the lid. Then they lowered the coffin into the grave. Steinar shovelled over the topsoil, and while he rested, Siegfried positioned the turfs of grass. He then placed nine white stones in a small cairn at the head of the grave.

Steinar packed away the tools. 'Tuva will come up later on with some flowers.'

Siegfried got into the tractor next to him. 'We will all stand here again when Anna is home.' The snow began to fall more thickly. 'I hope Anna finds what she is looking for. The forecast is bleak.'

The next day, Siegfried and Fridtjof met in the kitchen of the summer farm. Siegfried made a pot of coffee on the stove.

'It is freezing in here. Fridtjof rubbed his hands. 'What will Anna return to when she comes back? Why does she want to punish herself like this?' He paced around the kitchen. 'This is a farm for easy work in the summer. Some parts of it are comfortable enough in the autumn, but not when the place is man-deep in snow. We will not be nearby, either, to protect a lone woman, as I have said many times. The farmhouse needs renovation if she wants to stay.'

'As does my place, but I am too old to do it.' Siegfried opened the top of the coffee pot and smelled the aroma. He poured coffee into two mugs. 'Anna said she will be busy too, teaching at the school in Burfjord.'

Fridtjof was already shaking his head. 'How will she get to Burfjord? On your plough?'

Siegfried laughed. 'She's the toughest girl in the valley. She will walk and ski. Or maybe she will take over and drive the plough.'

Fridtjof disagreed more vehemently. 'She is not tough at all. I believe Gunnar's death has broken her spirit. She is not thinking clearly.'

Siegfried added a splash of his moonshine from his hip flask to the coffee. He offered some to Fridtjof, who declined. 'Emil is dead, and Anna is trying to get over it. Put yourself in her shoes. What would you do?'

Fridtjof sipped his coffee and dropped in a sugar cube from a bowl on the table. 'I hope she finds something on her journey, something that will heal the wounds.'

'She said goodbye to Emil three years ago; she didn't expect it to be their last goodbye.'

'She will see Emil again.' Fridtjof spoke more loudly.

Siegfried leaned in to make his point. 'My old friend, Anna does not take with talk of the afterlife.' He sat back in his chair.

Fridtjof sighed very deeply. 'I hate to see her in such pain, and at such a loss. Do you think she can really live here?'

Siegfried shrugged. 'Anna is a grown woman, an able farmer, an educated teacher, and a sensible person.' He took a sip of his coffee. 'She can make up her own mind.'

'But all the evidence is in front of her. This is a dilapidated place. She makes little from teaching, even less from the brunost she sells to tourists at the shop.'

'We must let her be. People are free to choose their own way.'

'Even if it's the wrong way?'

'Yes, especially if it's the wrong way.' Siegfried reached out and took away Fridtjof's coffee mug from in front of him, slopping some of the brown liquid on the counter. 'Would you like it if I arranged your life for you?'

There was silence between them for a moment. Fridtjof looked out of the kitchen window across to the fjord. Siegfried quietly finished his coffee.

'We should contact Birgit, her sister.'

'Why?'

'We will have an open discussion with her about how we can best help Anna, if indeed she wants any help. I will say, though, that the episode with Gunnar was troubling. She will surely have regretted it. But, as you say, Anna is her own person, that is for sure.'

'Birgit was sensible at the time of Emil's disappearance. She realised after a few days that there was little hope. The police inspector said as much. Birgit will want Anna to move on.' Siegfried returned Fridtjof's mug to the table. 'We all want Anna to be happy again, but we must present her with options, not decisions.' He turned the counsellor's business card around in his hand. 'This is our job now.'

CHAPTER 24

They roped up after the wall and walked on, Kristin beside her as they followed Lars. Kristin's camera hung around her neck, but she did not stop to use it. They carried on quietly for an hour or so walking along the flat plain, Anna willing the distance to disappear, and cursing the sight of Lars' back which nevertheless drove her on.

'Where are we? Where's the observatory?' she whispered to Kristin.

'He says he doesn't remember this exact route. But we just need to head north.'

When they stopped to huddle in the wind, Lars came back to stand with them. His eyes were dark pools under his hat. 'Things have changed,' he said. 'The land has shifted. That avalanche didn't help.' He walked away to look at some distant peaks and came back. 'We're parallel to the route I did a few days ago with Tomas.'

'Really? Are you sure?' asked Anna.

'The summit is up there,' and Lars pointed ahead of them into the white sky.

Anna peered to where he was pointing. 'I can't see anything.'

'The observatory is on the summit, and we're below it in another valley which leads us well away from the coast. Let's go and keep up.' He picked the rope up and walked off ahead of them.

Anna and Kristin walked quickly after him. 'We're lost, aren't we?' asked Anna.

Kristin smiled. 'We'll get there.'

'You don't seem very worried.'

'Should I be? We've got Lars.'

'You have a lot of faith in one person.'

'He's a good man. Look at all those badges on his jacket. He's an excellent guide. He's proved it before. He'll get us there.'

'Maybe, but perhaps we need some help.' Anna stopped.

'Maybe I can help.'

Kristin called out to Lars who came back to stand with them. 'Anna would like to lead.'

'Yes,' said Anna. 'I have also have a compass.'

'Why would that help?'

'Because you're lost, and I'm not stupid. I've also done this before.'

'OK,' said Lars. 'Go ahead.'

Anna looked at the needle on her compass. It spun around the casing with each shake of her hand.

'That way,' she said, pointing into the distance.

'No, that is away from the observatory. We need to go up.'

Anna looked again and struggled to make sense of the compass needle. 'I can't see which way is up. It all looks the same.'

'This is no time for tea and biscuits. We must move on. The weather is getting worse.'

'How much further?' asked Anna.

'Why do you ask? We won't get there any quicker.' Lars gazed at the sky that was turning from white to grey.

'There's been snow; maybe it's hidden the observatory?' said Kristin.

'Are there any huts in the area?'

'No, not up here. No one comes up here. This is the short cut compared to the coastal road which is longer and easier. Here, there are no snowmen or children playing snowballs. There's no cafe serving hot chocolate.' Lars turned away and walked on.

Kristin pulled a face at Anna. 'The best we can do is to follow him despite the uncertainty.'

So, this is my test, she announced to the snow, as if I haven't been tested enough. Very well. I have managed for three years in the face of adversity, and I will manage again. Me, the toughest girl in the valley.

The whiteness, the expanse of pure white snow and ice, the growing wind and storm, did not react to her determination.

She leant towards Kristin who turned to look at her. 'I'm not really going to visit my sister,' she said. 'She lives in Finland. I'm going to look for my missing husband.'

'I knew it was more than that.' Kristin waited to hear more.

'Emil never came back. He was lost on the coast somewhere near here. Taking photographs of the sunset. The police think he got surprised by the tide, disoriented in some way, that he must have drowned.' She sighed. 'Not that they found his body.'

Kristin put her arm around Anna's shoulder. 'We're taught, and I believe this is true, that we see our loved ones again in the next world.'

Anna shook her head. 'I don't think that can be true. Without our bodies how can we be anything?'

'So, you like to make things difficult for yourself, and not believe?'

Lars came over. 'We must be too far west. We will track towards the coast and get to Uektefjord that way. One way or the other I will get you to your sister.'

Kristin shook her head at Lars.

'Did I say something wrong?'

'Anna isn't visiting family at Uektefjord. Her husband went missing three years ago, walking on the coast.'

Lars looked at her, searching her eyes for more information. 'I see. Are we also in danger of going missing?' He pulled Kristin towards him.

Anna was incredulous. 'Do you think I murdered my husband? Do you think I'm a murderer?'

She sat down in the snow and began to cry. 'I've searched for Emil ever since the day he left. All our friends helped looked for him. The police tried everything. After a year they said there was little hope of finding him. For three years I denied that he was dead. I never gave up hope.' She hit the ground with a gloved fist. 'Then Gunnar, our dog, died and that was awful. All around me was death, my husband, dog, even the farm was falling apart, I was falling apart too.' She drew in a deep sob and exhaled a warm cloud of air. 'I searched everywhere, uncovered every stone, and found no clues. That's why I'm here, my last chance to find out what happened to him, to find some news of him, to find if someone knows something.' The tears were frozen in her eyes.

'And you think I'm his killer?'

Lars offered her his hand. 'No, Nansen, you are not a killer. Not after that reaction.'

Anna knocked his hand away. She lay down in the snow and looked up at the sky. She remembered her bed at the summer farm, remembered Gunnar as he lay asleep for the last time. Remembered the last kiss with Emil, so long ago.

Lars knelt beside her. 'I'm sorry,' said Lars. 'But strange things happen, and I have to protect Kristin.'

She lay in the snow a while. She had been the first suspect on Inspector Rohde's list, an honour automatically awarded to the spouse. The clouds in the sky said nothing to her. The wind, snow and ice were silent. The hills and mountains were just hills and mountains. Emil was still waiting somewhere and she wasn't going to find him laying here.

She rolled over on to all fours and stood up. 'Let's go,' she said, passing the rope between them. 'I'll lead so you can keep an eye on me.'

CHAPTER 25

They found another valley and a tongue off the glacier that pointed to the north. In the silence of their good luck, they stepped into skis and set off, hope rekindled. Then Anna saw something poking up out of the ground ahead of her, the only item of interest on the blank white page of the landscape.

The object that stuck out of the ice had a dark brown shank and a flat circle with a hole in it at one end. She touched the object carefully and found that it was made of metal, its texture rough with rust. She tugged, but the item was held fast in the snow. Emil's arrowhead came to mind; was this another weapon of war? With her ice axe, and Lars and Kristian waiting impatiently, she dug around the metal object. Digging only loosened the object a little. She sensed Lars' frustration and backed away from the object. 'After you.'

Lars bent down, wrapped a large gloved hand around the object, and pulled.

The thing came free in a cascade of snow. It was a metal hoop attached to a chain. 'It's a shackle,' said Lars. 'This is the key to tighten or loosen the binding. By the size of it, I'd say it would fit around the leg, or the neck.'

Anna looked wide-eyed at the object. 'What's it doing here?'

Lars shrugged. 'It's old.' He tested the key which did not turn. 'Rusted up.' He smoothed his hand down to the end of the chain. 'There is a post or other fitting missing.'

'What's it for?' asked Kristin.

'Tethering animals is my guess.' He smiled. 'I've heard stories of shackles being used to tether children to the cliff tops over the fjords to stop them falling over while they play.'

'I'm sorry,' said Kristin, 'but Lars is teasing you.'

She took the device and turned it over in her hands. 'So, this could be used for animals or men?'

'It's a shackle for reindeer, a throwback to the nineteenth

century.'

'It looks like an instrument of torture.' Kristin blew into her hands and hopped about to keep warm.

Anna laid the shackle out on the snow. She imagined the binding around Emil's leg. Her husband captured, kept in a cave, shackled by the leg to a post. His unknown captor or captors demanding what? Money, notoriety, the settling of a grudge? After what had happened on the island of Svindel, this remote area of Norway was not so safe anymore.

'Anna, I hope you are not thinking the worst?' Lars gave the shackle a tap with his boot. 'This thing has been rusted shut for many years. It has nothing to do with your husband unless he tripped over it in the ice.' He turned and walked away.

Kristian put an arm around Anna's shoulders. 'Lars sees the world in black and white.'

'As do I, no doubt.' Anna looked over the ice. 'The one interesting object I've found on this trip, and immediately it has something to do with Emil.'

'We cannot help but search for meaning.'

'That thing stuck up out of the ice, like the shard of glass I stepped in at home.'

Kristin was walking away. 'Look, Lars has found something else.'

Anna followed her to where Lars knelt on the snow, pawing at the ice like a dog. When they reached him, he turned around and presented something that gleamed in the light as much as his smile. 'Now, this is a real find!'

The object in his hand was a large blue goblet. Anna took it from him and turned the find over inspecting every aspect. 'It is a goblet, made from blue glass. Very pretty, with a design of leaves around the edge, although there is a chip on the rim.' She tapped the base. 'Solid work, not a cheap thing. It seems quite new.'

She handed the goblet to Kristin who mimed drinking from it. 'I guess this fell out of someone's backpack on their trek over the ice.' She handed the goblet back to Anna.

'Or it has been washed up here in the sea from miles away.' Lars shook his head. 'Is there a name on it?'

Anna looked at the base of the goblet then realised Lars was teasing her again. 'Of course not. It is a lucky find that is all.' Anna admired the goblet, a work of art that she appreciated as a practical drinking vessel, something she would test out with some brandy or wine when she next had the chance.

She wrapped up the goblet in her scarf ready to place in her rucksack. She hesitated, holding the bundle, and then unwrapped it to have another look.

'OK,' said Lars, 'let's go.'

But Anna had taken off her sunglasses and was staring at the goblet. 'Oh, I'm getting such a funny feeling.' Her eyes hurt with tears that froze as soon as they formed. She bent down, grabbed up a handful of snow, and rubbed it all over her face.

'Are you OK?' Kristin asked.

Anna nodded. 'What a blessed relief. This is amazing. To find anything out here at all.' She held the goblet up to the sun. 'This is exactly the sort of drinking vessel that Emil would have been interested in.' She inspected the goblet for any evidence that he might have touched it. Oh, Emil! Here I am, alone on the ice, and in my state, I dream all sorts of possibilities for this object. But my guides will tell me that I am merely a bereaved middle-aged woman embellishing random objects thrown up by the ice.

Kristin spoke softly. 'We need to get going. We have no tent so we cannot shelter on the ice.' Kristin stood even closer. 'Anna, we will be in real trouble if the storm hits.'

Anna didn't move. 'Gunnar's body had started to smell. I think that was the trigger for what I did. Death was beginning to upset my lonely life again.' Her voice was small. 'I tried to burn the body, and when that didn't work, I used lime.' She stood with shoulders sagging and head bowed. 'It is the worst thing I've ever done.'

'You were scared,' said Kristin, 'with no one there to help you.' She put an arm around her. 'Fear doesn't let you think straight.'

Lars clapped his hands twice in her face. 'Come on, Nansen. Remember that you were a hero today. If not for you, then that boy would have gone down the moulin.'

'I guess, the same thing could have happened to Emil.'

Anna drew exhaled several deep breaths feeling the tightness of he chest. 'That would make most sense.'

There was a misting of snow in the air, falling from a dark grey sky that now seemed to press down on them. They got ready to travel again. Lars pointed out a rocky peak. 'That's the summit of Stortfjell. The observatory is on the far slope.' Lars looked pleased with himself. 'After that, it's downhill all the way to the coast.'

Anna sighed. 'All I know is that the Hurtigruten ferry serves the best hot chocolate.'

Lars clicked his fingers. 'Of course. The ferry is still running and the other boats. We will look out for their lights.' Lars checked his watch. 'It's nine o'clock. We're nearer the end than the start. We will keep going.'

They stowed their skies and continued walking into the twilight that enveloped them and made the world smaller. For nearly an hour they walked, and then the way ahead rose steeply upwards and they burst through into open air. A rocky promontory jutted out above the mountains below. Lars walked to the very edge of the rocks with Kristin, and they stood there, shouting into the wind. The mists lay below them, wrapped around the lower peaks.

Anna felt a surge of energy in her chest as she joined them to shout her defiance and relief. Peaks down below rose out of the swirling mist like shark fins from the sea. She felt victorious, a conqueror, with a sense of being bigger than her problems. The moment faded but she took heart from the win, knowing that she could do more.

CHAPTER 26

Anna and Kristin rested at their vantage point, kings of the world. 'See the lights over there, the small village, that is Uektefjord. The larger village with lights out to sea, is Oksfjord.' She scanned the sea. 'No boats out, nothing big at least.' She sniffed the air. 'I think I can smell the sea.'

Kristin, huddled in her coat, managed a smile. 'You have an amazing spirit, Anna. You have been tested by life, and then doubted by us, and yet you are still standing.'

Lars arrived abruptly, sending snow up around his boots. 'Come and look at this.' He led them over a rise, to a hollow made in between two boulders of ice. They saw the bird on the snow, a grey and white grouse, its belly cut in two, lifeless eyes staring into space.

'There's more,' said Lars. 'Look at this!' He pointed to the markings in the snow. Four small pyramids of snow stood in a half circle of peaks, and at the apex, a flattened mound at the back of a large paw.

'A wolf?'

'What else?'

They heard barking and baying in the distance. Then three echoing cracks in the air.

'The wolves are trying to win a reindeer. The Sami must be nearby.' Lars looked down the mountainside, but nothing was to be seen.

'They're hungry,' said Anna. 'The Sami should give them an animal. Shoot a reindeer, not a wolf. Give them some food, keep them away from their people.'

'A sacrifice, you mean.'

'The reindeer are bred for meat. One given to the wolves makes no difference.'

'Cold and logical,' nodded Lars.

'Wolves are devils,' said Kristin, crouched on the ground, hugging herself.

'No, not devils, nor demons, just animals with a taste for

meat, doing what animals do. I've never heard of wolves being such trouble. Something must have disturbed them.'

'You're a wolf lover,' said Lars.

'A lycanthrope,' said Kristin. 'Give me strength.'

Anna knelt next to her. 'Let's not lose our heads. I've seen such behaviour with dogs. These wolves have been kept somewhere, and they've broken free. They aren't wild animals. They think we're food. They may have been kept as dogs, but people haven't understood them, or they've mistreated them. If they were wild, then they wouldn't think of us as meat.'

Kristin's face was pale and sweaty. 'You're on the side of the wolves?'

'You mean the wolves are victims.' Lars looked incredulous.

'We're all victims now,' said Anna.

'That's not much consolation to Kristin.'

'If people grew up and saw themselves properly, we wouldn't have these problems.'

Kristin got up. 'Come on,' she said, getting to her feet.

Anna caught hold of her. 'Are you alright to walk?'

'I'm feeling unwell but I'm not waiting to be sacrificed.' She picked herself up, huddled in her coat.

They trudged up the ice, Kristin with her arm around Lars. Anna walked behind them, looking out for the wolves. They moved higher, and the mountain fell away on either side.

'We should be safer now. The reindeer are much easier to find than us.'

'Except we don't have guns like the Sami.' Lars stopped and let Kristin sit down. He picked up Anna's walking stick. 'This will have to do.'

'There's a large overhang up there, it'll be some shelter from the wind.' Lars spoke quietly to Kristin, nuzzling in her neck, trying to persuade her to move again, but she would not. In the end he knelt, put her over his shoulders and carried her up to where the ice was carved into a hollow with an overhanging roof.

'Water,' croaked Kristin.

Anna shook her head at Lars. 'We have none.'

'I'll get some. There's meltwater running off the glacier

over there. Anna will look after you.'

'You'll be OK,' she said to Kristin as they watched him trudge downhill with the water bottles. 'Lars is organised and efficient.'

What it was that touched Anna's boot, she did not see, but she turned around sharply and gave a little shout.

'What is it?' cried Kristin.

'I don't know. Nothing, it's nothing.' But something nipped at her heel.

Kristin curled into a ball and lay down in the deepest corner of the bowl. Her eyes shone brightly.

At the best moment, when Kristin was feeling at her worst, the wolf returned to prey on the sick woman. It darted out of cover and knocked Anna off her feet. Then the animal came back to nuzzle at Kristin's neck as she tried to hide in the icy wall of the overhang.

'Hey!' shouted Anna as she got up, and Lars returned instantly. The wolf, grey and white, slunk sideways to regard him with yellow intelligent eyes narrowed in an expression of thought. Its ears, black with white insides, pricked up as it studied Lars. Then pain coursed through its body, or an injury flared up, or it was reminded somehow of its hunger, its status in life, its fight for survival, and the animal advanced a step and snarled.

Anna handed Lars her walking stick. Instead, he took the hammer out of his jacket and raised it above his head.

'The wolf's injured,' said Anna, 'he's been kicked out of the pack. A beta male, angry, and starving, look at his ribs.'

The wolf stood fearless, looking at Lars directly. It was caught between Kristin and Anna on one side and Lars on the other.

Lars raised his hammer. 'Away!' he roared. His voice reverberated in the chasm. The wolf stood its ground.

'Watch out,' said Anna. 'The wolf is ready to do or die.'

Then the wolf was at Lars, lunging and nipping at his ankles. He swung the hammer and caught the wolf on his hind legs. The wolf squealed and retreated, but darted back again, and scored a hit on Lars' leg.

Lars cried out in pain. The hammer fell in the snow.

Kristin got to her feet to try and reach it. The wolf turned back to her. Lars forgot his injury, and advanced on the wolf, bare-handed. The wolf turned on the spot, its mouth agape, Lars slipped, and the wolf bit his hands.

'Hey!' shouted Anna and she swung at the animal with the hammer. The animal dodged the blow, and snapped at her in a blinding move, biting her jacketed arm, on the way to scrabbling towards her neck. The hot breath of the animal on her face smelt of blood and guts. Anna fell back on the ground as the wolf lunged at her. Her hand tightened around the hammer and they all heard the metal on bone when it cracked the wolf's skull.

The wolf lay on the ground, seemingly frozen. Its jaws wide open, the rich red of its mouth glistening, its canine teeth inches long. The brown fur of its body gave way to the white fur of its face and the black of its lower jaw and nose. Its eyes were open, and through narrow slits, it gave the impression that it might spring into life at any moment. But the wolf lay still, and there was no rising of its head, like Gunnar used to do, interrupted from his sleep, so human-like, to have a look around, then to lie down again and nod off.

Anna knelt over Lars, who was trying to get up. 'Wait! Your leg is bitten.'

Lars stood up anyway. 'It's just a flesh wound.' He grimaced as he moved. 'You were brave, Nansen. You killed the beast.' He went over to inspect the dead wolf. Then he saw that Kristin was shaking. 'It's OK,' he said softly, hugging her to him. 'The wolf is dead.'

'It's the adrenalin. Freeze, run, fight; we are all different.' The wind had picked up enough strength now to muster a howl. 'We need to find shelter. We are too exposed up here.'

Lars pointed down the slope. 'There's an ice cave ahead. I remember it from before, with Tomas, near this summit.' He stopped to pick up his rucksack.

'No, go on. I'll get it. You look after Kristin.'

Anna followed her guides, slipping and sliding at points, managing three rucksacks and skis. 'Where's the cave?' she called. 'I can't see anything.'

'It's close by.'

'Where?' shouted Anna. 'Oh yes, is this it? Yes, this is the cave!' A blue portal opened in the white landscape.

They entered the cave, which was quite small, and Kristin collapsed with Lars on the floor.

'Is it safe?' asked Anna. 'Animals might live in here.'

'It's safe,' said Kristin, leaning against the wall. 'No animal will enter with a dead wolf outside.' Then she crouched down on her haunches in pain.

Anna looked out of the entrance. 'I can't see anything.'

'You won't, and nothing will see us, not in this storm. We're well hidden.'

Anna watched at the entrance, fearful of other wolves attacking, but Kristin rested, seemingly unworried, and soon Anna was heavy with fatigue. She rested next to Kristin, and trusted she was right.

The blue of the cave walls deepened the further they explored, changing from azure around the entrance to a deep cobalt in its depths. Anna took off her glove and touched an icicle. It felt hot at first, and then cold, as the ice melted and ran over her hand. 'Look at the walls. They look good enough to eat, like sorbet or meringue. Isn't that strange?' She stood up and stepped towards the cave's depths. 'It's like looking into an aquarium or a fishbowl. Are you sure nothing lives in here?'

'Nothing for us to worry about,' said Lars. 'Not while we have Nansen, wolf-destroyer, with us.'

Anna looked around. 'This is an amazing place, made of ice and light.'

'Pretty as a snowflake, no wolf will come in here.'

Kristin was yawning. 'I feel sick,' she said. Lars sat her on his rucksack and wrapped his coat around her shoulders. 'Food poisoning, maybe. She needs a rest.' After a while, Kristin closed her eyes, and went to sleep.

Anna stayed wide awake. She could not sleep even if she wanted to, and she was not at all sure why a wolf would not enter the cave. She picked up their skis and stood them up against a wall where icy water dripped down their shining lengths onto the floor. She took off her sweater, rolled it up and placed it under Kristin's head as a pillow.

Lars looked pale. He let her inspect the bite marks on his leg and hands. 'You must get these seen to,' she told him, 'a tetanus shot. You know that.' He nodded, his eyelids droopy, and soon both of her guides were asleep, Kristin curled up into a ball, hands on her belly. Lars was flat out on his back, arms by his side where he had been laid, his long legs extended across the width of the cave.

Anna wondered about wolves and rabies. Lars had many cuts on his hands as well as the puncture wounds in his calf. She undid his boots, carefully picking undone his laces, then she tried to loosen the boots to take them off. The boots stayed on, immovable, as Lars slept. Anna gave up and sat back against the ice wall. She yawned and looked up to the top of the cave. A blue light radiated around the walls, and for some reason, even though the wind howled outside, she felt safe. She turned the hammer over in her hand, then fell asleep.

CHAPTER 27

T he three travellers slept, hidden from the wind. Kristin called out in her sleep, but neither Lars nor Anna heard her moan. Anna slept with her head fallen forward on her chest.

She dreamt of a tall man, with strong hands, who picked her up and sat her on his shoulders and held onto her ankles as they walked along. The trek was easy, through beautiful scenery: mountains capped with snow, silvery trails of glaciers easily conquered, a summit in the clouds with strange birds overhead, a lush green hillside on the way home, and then the first sight of the sea, shimmering before her as they reached the beach. And then she was left on a rock, with the fleeting glimpse of the man leaving down the path, and a soft crying coming from her mother at the window.

Anna shouted and woke up. Kristin stirred on the floor and opened an eye. 'What is it?'

Anna patted her jacket and her trousers, embarrassed by her fright. She looked at Kristin. 'Nothing,' she said. She looked at Lars' body. He was lying on his front, arms resting up around his head, feet turned out, giant boots kicked off on the snowy floor. She got up and saw that he was awake with a smile on his face.

'How's the leg?'

'Hurts like hell.' He turned over, sat up and inspected his hands. 'A wolf should really kill a man, not tickle him.'

Lars looked older. His beard was blunted, and his hair matted. His eyes met Anna's and a smile played across his face. 'Nansen, you are our new leader.' Then he turned his attention on the entrance. 'The snow has blocked us in. I'll clear it.' Lars stood up, hobbled to where the entrance had been and, without hesitation, dropped his shoulder and bulldozed into the drift. He pushed a way through the wall of snow with his bare hands. Part of the roof of the cave came down in the process turning the floor of the cave a lighter colour.

They stepped outside. All was quiet outside the cave under the midnight sun. The snow glowed blue in places like the wells in the glacier. They listened to the silence and let their eyes adjust to the peaceful light off the snow.

'Come on,' said Anna, 'we're nearly there. Soon we will have food, water and warmth.

Lars supported Kristin while taking their rucksacks and skis on his back. Anna had her compass and was waiting to move on. Snow began to fall. She clapped her gloves together. 'It's much colder now.' She looked at Lars. 'Another couple of hours do you reckon?'

'Of course, if that,' said Lars, glancing at Kristin. 'It is easy now. Uektefjord is in the distance. Follow the valley to the sea. When we get low enough, we will turn for the crossing to Oksfjord and say our goodbyes.'

'If there is a boat running at this time?'

'There is always a boat.'

Kristin stood swaying as powdery snow swirled around her feet. 'We must go now. I have little energy for another fight.'

They set off, trudging downhill. Anna was suddenly full of thoughts of Fridtjof, Siegfried, Brigit, and her nieces. I have disappeared just like Emil. A missed phone call one evening, and what will people have thought?

Slowly, the three travellers descended from the summit heading for the coast. The way was tricky in places, with slippery rocks, made more difficult with the heavy loads on their backs. She looked at Lars as he carried twice the load, uncomplaining, and guided Kristin down the glacier. Crampons trudged on ice, snow, and rock, and over the next two hours the coast came slowly closer.

'Look!' shouted Anna. She pointed to a building the size of a hut on the hill. 'Is that the observatory?'

'That's it!' said Lars. 'We've found it!'

'It's a peculiar design.' Anna stopped and looked up at the building, which was shaped like a ship's funnel, or a periscope. 'It's obviously for looking out of.' She laughed a little. 'It's some sort of joke, very funny.' They approached the building and found the entrance at the back. Inside, a short flight of steps led up to a viewing platform where she peered out of the funnel's aperture. 'We should stop here to rest. It's an observatory after all; you could watch the weather or the lights here.'

Lars brought Kristin inside the observatory, where Anna heard her tearful thanks for helping her along. Lars climbed up the stairs, and joined Anna looking out of the funnel. They inspected the coastline and saw the lights of moving boats far away on the water. She gazed for a long time, thinking that she was her journey's end, until she realised Lars had gone.

'He's out collecting firewood.' Kristin shivered in her jacket on the stone bench. 'He says I need to get warm before the last push to the coast.'

'The weather is getting worse, but I agree. I am hungry as well.' Kristin looked tired to Anna. Her face had lost its colour.

The smell of wood smoke reached them. Lars was outside bending over a fire set in the middle of a circle of stones. 'That's quick,' she called.

'Come and sit here to block the wind, or we will have nothing to eat.'

A metal pot filled with boiling water stood on its legs over the fire. Lars took three packets of instant noodles out of his rucksack, tore the tops off with his teeth, and dropped the contents into the pot. Their meal cooked in the time it took the mountains behind him to change colour from blue to purple.

They joined Kristin inside, and sat together on the stone bench, collars up, hoods and caps on, Anna and Lars taking turns to eat the noodles out of the pot. When they were finished Lars went outside to boil up more water and returned with a pot of beef stock. The hot drink flooded Anna with warmth from her neck to her toes. Anna wanted nothing but the warmth of the cooking pot wrapped up in Lars jacket, which she hugged to herself. For a moment they were able to forget the wind and cold which was beginning to bite.

'How long to go?' asked Kristin.

'No more than a couple of hours, my love.'

Kristin groaned and Lars looked worried. 'It is really cold

now, double digit freezing. 'We should move on.'

They cleaned their bowls in the snow and kicked over the fire. The cooking pot was plunged into snow to cool it down. Everything was packed away into Kristin's rucksack which Lars carried. Then they stood ready to go. Only a flurry of snow in the air warned them of what was to come.

Anna looked back to the mountain behind her. 'We have come a long way. What a tale to tell!'

Lars and Kristin stood, swaying together, he with her weight, rucksack, and skis. 'A great tale indeed, Anna, and not for nothing.'

The weather was getting worse. 'OK, let's go.' Anna looked around at the greyness that suffocated the place. The compass needle pointed ahead, twelve o'clock, to north. Always north, to the land of Hyperborea, where all your troubles will disappear.

'It's a gentle trip downhill all the way. Then we will have our rewards and our biggest fantasies.

'A hot bath in the hotel at Oksfjord,' said Kristin.

'I have the same fantasy,' said Lars.

Anna led the way, her eyes fixed on the coast. A beach, she thought. She would believe it when she saw it. Kristin walked for a while, but then Lars carried her on his shoulders, a rucksack in either hand. They moved along as a group, kicking up the snow, the wind rising, calling, teasing, forcing their heads down.

They almost collided with the tall stone man that stood in their path. The dark grey statue was three metres high, with thin legs and a thin body, a giant with a big nose, rudimentary eyes and mouth, but no ears. He held out his hands and all ten fingers and thumbs pointed upwards like little solders. He looked up and away into the sky. Whatever he was offering, or was hoping to receive, was not clear.

They all stopped and gazed up at the statue. 'Am I hallucinating?' asked Kristin.

'No, he is really here.' Anna saw that her guides seemed worried. Lars had the same fierce look when he took on the wolf, eyebrows lowered over his eyes, leaving only slits of white as a target. 'Who has done this? How did we miss this before?'

'Has it just appeared?' Anna walked all around the tall stone man. 'It seems friendly.'

Snow began to settle around them in earnest as the light began to fade. The dark clouds snuffed out all the light spaces in the sky. Their world became quieter.

'The sky goes dark, and now arrives the season of blizzards. The fire in the air will be of no use.' Kristin huddled in her jacket where she was sat on Lars' shoulders.

'Darling wife, you need a dull imagination, like mine.' Lars gave the tall stone man a kick as he passed. 'Let's go. At least it's not a head on a pole. We need to get to the coast or find shelter.'

They were crossing an exposed plain when the blizzard hit. At first, snow appeared in the blustery wind, whipping around them. Then the wind strengthened and became a stream of cold white air. All around was the dreadful sound of Boreas howling across the ice.

Their words were ripped apart in the wind. Lars and Kristin knelt and began digging up the snow, remaking it into a low wall to shelter behind. They managed a wall of about a metre high and three metres long. Lars produced a small orange bag from his rucksack. He unfolded it carefully, with Kristin holding onto it, as the wind picked up and tried to take them away. Anna recognised the bivouac bag; it would offer some shelter from the wind, but it looked big enough for only two people. Kristin slid into the bag gracefully and lay down behind the low wall.

Lars put his mouth up to Anna's ear. 'Get into the bag.' She did so, struggling in next to Kristin, and wondered what Lars was to do as there was no room for his big body. Lars slid one leg into the bag and turned to face her, his arms around Anna, so that he could touch Kristin. Anna closed her eyes. She lay with Lars and Kristin in the orange wind-sack like rubbish waiting for disposal. It felt strange to have a man so close to her again, but it was not an unpleasant feeling. Lars had his hood pulled over his head. He must be so cold; he was barely in the bag. She pulled on his jacket and brought him closer to her. 'The storm will not last long,' shouted Lars in her ear.

There was no way he could know that, but she appreciated the effort.

Soon it became very warm in their shelter, as they shared body heat between each other. They listened to the wind build and push at them, at one point bowling over the rucksacks and sending the skis to the ground. Then the snow whirled over their heads and they realised that the wall had given way. They ducked further into the orange bag and crowded together. Kristin, Anna realised, was praying. She wrapped her leg around Kristin's to let her know that there was some hope. Boreas could not keep this up for long and then they would reach Uektefjord and her trek would be over.

Then she thought of Emil and his final moments, and what he would have been thinking and whether there had been any chance to survive.

CHAPTER 28

B irgit arrived at the farm and the first thing Nina and Solveig did was to look for the goats in the orchard, but they were disappointed.

'We moved Silje and her sisters down to my farm,' said Fridtjof. 'Alva and Tuva have taken over the milking and making cheese.' He explained to Birgit what he knew of Anna's disappearance. 'She is a stubborn woman, determined to stay here in the winter until Emil returns.'

'Every winter since Emil disappeared my sister used to say she would die on this farm rather than move anywhere warmer. Always it was about it being our parents' farm. Or she didn't want to be away if Emil showed up. In the end, when winter came, it was a week here and a week at mine. That was her way of finding a balance.'

Birgit talked with Fridtjof as they walked through the farmhouse. 'Emil's things are still here, of course.' She admired his photographs on the walls. 'He was such a lovely man, so creative.' She stopped at the large dog basket and noticed the silver food and water bowls washed up near the sink. 'Brave Gunnar kept my sister company for a long time. The lone dog with the lone wolf.'

They went outside. Fridtjof inspected the building and pointed out where insulation could be laid, or improvements made. He hung equipment he found on the ground back on the walls, repositioning tree loppers and secateurs neatly on hooks, and tied back the thorny stems of a flowering rose bush that had gone astray.

'This place is as I remember it from childhood.' Birgit opened the lid of the metal post box on the side of the farmhouse and looked inside. She dropped the lid with a clang. 'It is the same noise, of course. Why should it be different.' She stepped back and looked at the wooden farmhouse built on a brick surround and topped with a corrugated roof. Where the black stove pipe exited the roof, she saw something new.

'There's one.'

'One what?' Fridtjof looked up to where she was pointing.

'See that short grey tube next to the stove pipe? It is a pin-hole camera made from a beer can. Emil made them for the girls. He put one up on our house, too. We developed it a few months after he went missing: a very pretty picture, with the sun arcing across the sky. If Anna hasn't moved this one for three years, it will either be a masterpiece, or an overexposed mess.'

Siegfried joined them, and when he found out about the camera, placed a ladder against the wall of the building. Despite protests about his age, he climbed the ladder, undid the tape around the beer can and brought it back down. He un-peeled the grey plastic to reveal a can of Mack. 'Emil liked the local brew, that is a good sign.' There was a piece of black card wrapped around the outside and taped up with black tape to form a cap.

Birgit showed him the pinhole. 'The light comes in here and falls on a piece of photographic film. Then the film is de-veloped, somehow.'

Siegfried put the can in his pocket. 'I will find out what to do with this. We will see what Emil's last photograph looks like.'

Nina and Solveig came to join them, and they walked through the deserted orchard, past the trees with hanging fruit, and out across the pasture to Gunnar's grave. 'Poor Gun-nar, poor Anna.' Birgit wiped her eyes with the end of her sleeve, her daughters crying by her side. 'So much pain for my sister. It really is not fair.'

'Too much pain for one person to bear alone.' Fridtjof lowered his voice so that the girls could not hear. 'We are here for her, but she has gone and run away.'

'She is out there looking for him.' Birgit crossed herself at Gunnar's grave. 'It is something she must do.'

They returned to the farmhouse and made them-selves comfortable around an old wooden table and chairs weathered by the elements. Siegfried brought out a jug of warmed apple juice and a bowl of plums. They did up their jackets as the cold wind blew.

'Thank you for all you have done,' said Birgit. 'I will talk with Anna when she gets back. We must make sure she moves on from this moment.' Her daughters sipped at their apple juice in silence. 'Last year we asked for three evaluations on the farm. I thought Anna was going to sell, but because Emil was not officially deceased, it was more complicated.' She paused. 'That would have been too much for her. But now I will ask for updated figures.

'I'd like Anna to come and live with us,' said Solveig.

'We would like it too. She also talked about leasing out the farm for someone else to run.' Birgit looked over the land. 'I was surprised at first by such talk. Our parents farmed here for a long time, and she has such a strong link to the place. We played here as children in the summers; it was perfect.'

'Alva knows the principal at the school in Burfjord,' said Fridtjof. 'She says the school will close in the next two years. There are not enough local children in the area. Anna would do better in a bigger town or city.'

Birgit agreed. 'The school closure has been on the cards for a while.'

Siegfried held his hands up. 'This is not a coup. Our friend has left her house to find what happened to her missing husband. The moment she is gone, we are dreaming up ways to change her life. We agreed to offer Anna possible solutions, not final decisions. We are not taking the farm from her. If she wants to stay here in the winter that is her business, and I for one will try and help her make the place hospitable.'

The wind began to throw fat raindrops across the garden towards them. They retreated inside to the living room. Birgit inspected the photographs and settled on one of a woman wearing a traditional black dress and long white blouse with a girl stood by her side. 'That's me with my mother when I was little. I passed that red jacket on to Nina.'

Birgit sat in the rocking chair. 'And this was mother's chair.' She rocked back and forth. 'How she would laugh to see me now. Anna and I always fought over whose turn it was to have her chair.'

Solveig picked up a thick book: *Norges Helltopper*. 'Grandpa's book.'

'Correct. There is his picture on the wall.' Solveig went over to look at a handsome man in a suit and tie framed in a long oval portrait. 'A wonderful man, strong and kind, although too strong for my mother.' She let her girls run around the farmhouse finding more old photographs and smiled at their giggles when they recognised their mother.

Fridtjof was sat on the sofa while Siegfried was leafing through a book on photography.

Birgit rocked slowly back and forth. 'There is magic in this chair. I can see why Anna would want to stay here.'

CHAPTER 29

In her sleep, Anna felt hands moving around her waist. She was sure there had been a kiss on her cheek. Emil is that you?

She snapped awake. The comforting warmth of Lars and Kristin in the bivvy bag were gone. She rolled over on to her knees, hiding her face from the blizzard. The rucksacks and skis remained, covered in snow. She got to her feet with the orange bag tied by a safety line to her waist.

'Lars! Kristin!' She could not believe that her guides had gone, without even saying goodbye. Perhaps Lars had got too cold? Perhaps Kristin had become ill? They had left their rucksacks; none of it made sense. Anna stopped and tried to look and listen in the blizzard. Perhaps wolves had returned?

Her hand came away with a surprise gift from around her neck: Kristin's scarf. She stared at the purple snatch of material and wrapped it around her throat, tucking the hood of her jacket in for extra warmth. The wind blew snow in her face as she stood at the top of the slope and looked down to Oksfjord.

A movement near the statue caught her eye. The tall stone man was moving. She backed away as she saw it reach out for her. Then the giant man landed face down in the snow with a thud. She waited for other movement, for whoever had pushed the statue. 'Kristin! Lars!' she shouted. 'Where are you?' She walked up to the fallen statue, fighting through the blizzard, snow stinging her eyes, until she could touch its solid mass.

'Lars, Kristin. Where are you?' she called. Then she heard a sound in the wind above. She tried to look up, to search the sky. All she could see was white flakes coming down. Two animals, which she later would swear were two white horses, ran past her.

The snow wrapped around Anna, forcing itself on her, weighing her down. How could there be horses here? And who was responsible for the standing stones? Something soft brushed her face. 'Hello!' she called. She sheltered behind the giant man and shouted again for her guides: 'Lars! Kristin!' Her words were lost on the wind, which flapped orange plastic in her face. She tried to wrap the bivouac bag around herself, but it was too big and annoying, so she undid the safety line and let the shelter blow up away, soaring into the blizzard.

Boreas blew at her and pushed her back down on her knees. She crawled behind the giant man, grateful for the hiding place. In the lee of the ten fingered hands, she bent over the compass and tried to take a reading. Each time she tapped the compass, the needle settled on a position for a moment but refused to stay still. She edged further and further away from the statue, retreating backwards on her knees, as if leaving the presence of a great king. Finally, the needle stayed still and showed her north. She peered out into the storm, snow stinging and lancing into her eyes through the small gap under her hat. The path ahead, she worked out, was past the giant man and on towards a gap in the mountains that reared up to the west of Uektefjord.

She crawled over to her rucksack and thought about what she needed: water bottle, food, the first aid kit from Lars' rucksack. She looked up and set off on a path aiming for the gap in the mountains, swaying as the wind hit her, dropping to her knees when it was too strong, waiting for the worst to pass. She would have to take her chances and hope to find some shelter down the mountainside out of reach of the storm. The wind blew the snow across her path, rippling the white drifts like waves on the sea. Then the wind gusted, and puffed out the sides of her clothes, and cut into her bones.

The wind was so cold, it had radiance. She was bathed in white light: white-out, no shadows, no horizon, no depth, nothing but pure white light.

She lost a glove, and her fingers stiffened in the cold like frozen sticks. A tremble and a shudder ran down her neck from shoulders to her toes. The sky was blue and grey, lit by the hidden sun, the land merged with the snow-filled air. She lost her sense of up and down as she stumbled forward in large steps, as if climbing stairs, anxious about where to put her feet, not knowing where she would tread.

The gap between the two mountains had disappeared. Her hand was dying on the end of her arm. She started to run. Her boots took her downhill in a rush, her boots jarring on solid rock and ice or plunging into deeper snow. She fell and got up many times. Further down the valley was the hope of shelter, with each blind step forward she had a chance to survive.

A gust of wind knocked her over and pressed down, forcing her into the snow and ice. She stayed still, a smaller target for the wind. Fine snow whipped across her body, and she began to sink into the ground. If she stayed here, the edges of her body would disappear, and she would be slowly erased by the powdery white paint. Her left hand was a cold stone against her face.

Lyrics from the radio came back to her. The Cold Genius in Purcell's King Arthur, struggling to rise from an everlasting bed of snow. She could scarcely move or draw a breath. Then the last kiss with Emil revived her, and she felt again the warmth of his lips and his body.

She stood up and dared Boreas to knock her over again. The snow slid off her body as she patted down her arms and legs. A shape appeared in the distance.

She peered into the mirage of light and shadows. 'Lars! Kristin!' she called, then she ducked down as the wind threatened to pick her up. The shape was large and bulky, moving slowly towards her. She squinted into the storm as the shape approached, and then she ran, not knowing why, falling over, ditching the rucksack. There was the roar of the ocean, and the wind knocked her flat on her back, plunged her face first in the snow, scraping her cheek on the rock as she fell. Trees fell around her, lit up by lightning flashes. A huge thunderclap above her, and she thought the sky had split apart.

She struggled to get up and turn over, but she sank further into the snowdrift. She brought her arms and legs together and pulled her body into a ball, clearing space around her mouth to breathe. She waited, panting like a sick dog in the snow, waiting at the behest of her master to see whether she would be kicked again.

Boreas pinned her to the ground and did not relent. She pawed at the ground, her gloved hand clawing at the snow as she began to dig. She scratched the surface, and powder flew about her, but she persevered and struggled and reached firmer, more compacted snow. She forced herself to calm down, but the cold took her breath away and stung her throat and lungs. She spluttered and cried out, scooping the snow out of the deepening hole in a frenzy, her bad hand dead by her side.

She made the hole large and deep enough to sit in and she sank down up to her waist, legs up to her chest, hands over her head. The wind pushed up snow to cover her; she had made her own grave. Soon she would be no more than a pair of red eyes peering out underneath the rim of a hat.

The shape was moving in front of her. She was up and out of the hole and gone. She stumbled forward, away from the dark shape in the storm. Her steps were difficult, legs plunging into the snow; she had to wade as if crossing a river. She heard the creak of the snow as the ground beneath her gave way. She dropped with a scream that hurt her throat, but her boots hit solid ice, and she realised she stood at the start of a crevasse, with her head poking above the surface.

The wind relented; no more snow blew in her face. She shivered against the ice and snow that surrounded her, and tried to climb out, but did not have the strength in her arms.

'Help!' she shouted. 'Lars help me! Kristin, where are you?'

She looked out of the hole she was stuck in and tried to climb out again. Her legs and arms struggled and flapped, and she fell back in. She began to cry but the tears froze in her eyes.

In the swirling light, the shape moved nearer.

Anna ducked her head down into the hole and waited. Then she peeked up over the rim. The snow swirled around her, but she saw the dark shape a few metres beyond her, searching, looking for its prey.

She sat down in the hole, and relaxed, warmth spreading around her waist, and down her legs. Her muscles were soft.

She stopped shivering. Even her left hand, swollen red and purple, had a strange warmth. Her breath quietened.

This does not feel like Valium or like falling asleep; this is not a warm bath. I am not made of stone; I am made of flesh and blood. The cold is searching for a way into my jacket, making my lungs ache, looking to stop my heart. The warmth is an illusion preparing me for the end.

She tried to move her legs, but the message only reached her knees. She was relaxing and growing warmer; she was comfortable in her new hole. She could stay here and sleep the deepest sleep. She had no complaints that her life span would be shorter than some, but longer than others. I really wanted to see Emil again; I couldn't give him up. I did my best to find him, but I was foolish at the end with the risks I took.

CHAPTER 30

A shadow passed over the top of the hole, and the shape appeared before her, blocking out the light. Her hands came up in front of her face to meet the attack. But when the touch came, it was from a gloved hand.

There was fire in her arms and shoulders when the man pulled Anna out of the crevasse. He lay her down on the snow as gently as he could. 'Hello,' he said, and she tried to answer but no sound came out. The wind howled for the last time, pushed a spray of snow over her as it departed.

The man spoke again to her, and she watched his mouth move, understanding slowly. Then a younger man emerged from out of the snow, wearing a white bearskin and a tall red hat, and stood by her rescuer. In his arms was a husky, who jumped down and wrapped itself up into a small furry swirl on the snow next to Anna, its snout hidden in its coat. She was shaking and could not stop, a mixture of cold and relief. Her rescuer had a tanned, weather-worn face with a broken nose. She tried to talk, but her teeth and tongue would not cooperate.

The rescuer gave instructions and the younger, hatted man returned with a line of huskies pulling a long sledge covered in animal pelts. She felt hands under her head, and her back and legs, and then her rescuer and his companion lifted her up, head loose on her neck, and lay her down on the sledge.

They examined her face, touched her neck, looked into her eyes, as she lay on her back on the sledge. The younger man saw her exposed hand and looked at the swollen, blackened fingers, the red cracked skin running from fingertips to wrist. 'Forfrysning,' he said, and squeezed her fingers. Anna let out a little cry of pain. She watched as he took out a silver tube and squeezed a soft white cream onto her palm and fingers. Then he unwrapped a roll of beige bandage and wrapped it around her fingers and over her hand. He gave her a large fur glove to wear over the dressing.

The older man picked up the husky and placed it on Anna's lap. The animal looked at her with dark eyes. She was fully awake now.

'Sam-ah?' she said to the man.

He nodded. 'My name is Kauppi. Where are you going?'

'Uektefjord. To the beach'

He nodded. 'To the sea.'

He called out and several other red-hatted men emerged. The huskies sitting in the snow by their sledges, tongues lolling, were hitched up to their sledges.

There was a roar as one of the men boarded a snow scooter and rode out in front, the modern Sami in front of the traditional. Anna's rescuer marshalled his huskies and they sprang up, barking, pulling at their chains. Anna pulled the pelt covering her up to her neck, a goatskin, white and soft and warm. She held onto the sides of the sledge. With a shake of the reins and a click of his tongue the driver had the sledge away, pulled by five pairs of yapping dogs. The sledge hissed along over fields of snow, heading gently down through trees, Anna looking ahead and over her driver and his team. The sky lightened as they travelled, leaving the storm behind. The snow on the huskies' coats melted into their fur.

The air grew warmer, and trees appeared again with leaves cleaned of the snow. Huge lumps of snow fell from creaking and cracking branches. Dreams of the mountain fell away as the land grew flatter. Sami men were running through the snow behind them, led by the white bear-skinned man who strode through the snow, boots sinking then rising, almost as quickly as the sledge.

There was a noise on the wind now, a choir carried between the leaves and branches of the trees. Her face widened with delight when she saw the sea and the view beyond fell into relief. A large flock of birds called above them, dumpy birds with white bellies, small black wings, short legs, and large, triangular bills brilliantly coloured in yellow, blue and vermilion. The puffins flew over their heads, barrelling through the sky like uncertain missiles towards the fjord and their fishing grounds.

Their descent flattened and with a jolt the sledge came

off the end of the glacier tongue. Some of the Sami kept up with the sledge as her driver navigated the highs and lows of the slope heading to the sea, down the grassy plain to Uektefjord. The snow scooter who had scouted their path had stopped, and its rider waved to her, and she waved back. Other Sami stopped and unhitched their huskies and turned their sledges around waiting for her rescuer to complete his mission.

Another machine came up the hillside, a red quad bike with four large wheels and a roaring engine, pulling a red trailer, and stopped at her sledge. The Sami driving smiled at her and killed the engine. Again, she felt arms under her, and she was lifted from the sledge into the trailer. The quad bike started up again, slowly turned in a circle and moved downhill.

The driver of her sledge, Kauppi, the man who had pulled her out of the snow, sat next to her, holding her steady as they bumped along. Behind her, she said goodbye to the snow and ice, and was pleased to do so. Thoughts of Lars and Kristin intruded: where were her guides? She tried to ask Kauppi, but the noise and jostling of the trailer as it bumped downhill made it impossible. And she was distracted by the sea. The sky widened and flattened out, and she felt the breath of sea air on her face. I did it, she thought, I just needed a little help at the end. Behind her the land rose into an arduous climb back to Stortfjell. She hoped that Lars and Kristin were safe, and perhaps somehow, they had been rescued.

They slowed as they descended a steep track down to the fjord. The sea was sparkling, and the ground retained its summer greenery. Kauppi pointed to a large building on the left. When she saw the villa, her mouth fell open. The magnificent structure stood glistening in fine white wood. Faint patterns of yellow and blue played over the balconies and porches, and up the pillars and posts. Skewed rhombi of pale light spread from the windows and fell on the grass around the villa.

Berkeley's villa, and I thought people were joking.

Her driver delivered her down the track to the rear of the villa. Kauppi helped Anna out of the trailer where she stood clutching him for support. 'I'm cold,' she said, and then she felt a sudden wooziness, almost like fainting, come over her.

Kauppi knocked on the door, and a young woman came out of the villa. She had a long beautiful face.

'Who is this?' she asked.

Kauppi stood with Anna. 'A traveller from across the mountains.'

'You're in a bad way. Look at you, half-frozen, your clothes are torn.' The woman touched her bandaged. 'She can stay with us. Come inside and get warm.'

Anna took Kauppi's hand and he led her inside. Brown wood, old oak balconies were the first feature she recognised. Not Scandinavian at all, she thought, but old European. The woman led her up the stairs, and when she was at the top, she realised that Kauppi had gone. My hero, she thought, and I haven't even thanked him.

The young woman opened a door and led her into a bedroom. 'You must rest.' Anna lay down on the bed and the covers were pulled over her. 'Let me take these boots off. Now sleep, and I will be back later.'

When Anna woke, she took her time to think about where she was. She looked around the room lit by the glow of the sun around the window. The walls were wooden, painted dark green, the wooden roof a light cream. There was a small fireplace with a blue hearth and a white chimney, while the chairs were upholstered in a red fabric that matched the curtains. On the walls were mounted old wooden skis; snowshoes hung by the window.

The sea, she reminded herself. She tried to get up to draw back the curtain, but every part of her was aching and she lay back down. The thick fur glove bulked large on her hand. She closed her eyes and remembered the glacier, the blizzard, fighting with the wind, thinking she would die.

There was a knock on the bedroom door. Anna managed to call out a welcome. A familiar woman entered carrying a tray of food. Anna noticed her good looks, an ancestry of east and west.

'Hello, how are you feeling? I hope you're comfortable here.'

'Yes, thank you,' she said through dry lips.

'My name's Therese. I was with you when you arrived.'

She watched Therese lay the table with plates of food and a steaming drink. 'I'm Anna.'

'Hello, Anna. You were caught in a bad storm. The cold got to you. How is your hand?'

Anna thought about her hand in the glove. 'Stiff and sore, it throbs a bit.' She lifted her arm slowly and flexed the glove.

'At least you can feel it, That's a good sign.' Therese offered her a cup from the tray and Anna took it with her good hand. She tasted the hot red liquid. 'Cloudberry?'

'Cloudberry and apple.' Therese opened the curtains and the room filled with light.

Anna saw the sea and the curve of the coast. She remembered the place; it was not a fjord at all, but a bay. 'Is there really a golden beach?'

Therese stood by the window. 'Yes, a novelty for the area.' She paused and smiled a little. 'The owner, Berkeley, liked its ebb and flow so much he struck on this place for his meetings. The beach is uncovered at low tide.'

'The sea looks lovely now, so blue.'

'And warm, it is surprisingly mild here for this time of year; something to do with the Gulf Stream. When you've recovered, I'll show you around.'

A snowy dust breathed against the glass, blown from the roof. Yes, Boreas, I know you wait for me, but not even you can knock this villa over.

Therese went over to the tray and poured some milk over a bowl of sugar-crusted cornflakes. She prepared two slices of thick toast with butter and marmalade and set the tray in front of Anna on the bed. But Anna wasn't thinking about food.

'My guides. I had guides over the glacier. They disappeared.'

Therese sat at the end of the bed. 'From the glacier school? I can give them a ring.'

'Please. They were Lars and Kristin, I don't know last names, but they were married. Such a couple to make you proud. They put up with me for a long way.'

Therese spoke on her phone. 'I've had to leave a message. The storm caused some damage in Oksfjord.'

Anna remembered further back. 'And there was a boy, Marco, I stopped him drowning in a moulin.'

'I see we have a hero staying with us. What else?'

But Anna was crying, and Therese stood to comfort her and offer her tissues.

'I'm sorry, I've had such a time of it.' Anna blew her nose and rested her head on the pillow.

'I will make enquiries again at the glacier school and the medical centre in Oksfjord, but first let's get the dressing changed.' Therese took off the glove and unwound the bandages on Anna's hand. She held the tip of each finger. Anna winced each time she did. Then she leant down and sniffed the hand. 'No decay. Hopefully, you will not need a splint or anything more serious.'

She wet a flannel in the sink, wiped each finger clean of cream and blood, then dried each finger in the folds of a white cotton towel. 'I'll put on some more cream and a new dressing. The red sores should go down. Be careful with your hand even with the glove on. You will lose the skin if you are too rough.'

'I remember now,' Anna said. 'The Sami rescued me.'

'Kauppi is the one you should thank, and his sons. He is chief of the Sami in this area.' Therese rolled up the old dressing and put it to one side on the tray.

Anna became agitated, trying to sit up and get out of bed. 'There was a wolf. It attacked Lars. Kristin was so scared.' Then she sat still and looked puzzled. 'I killed the wolf.'

'OK. I see you need to rest; I should go.'

'No, please don't go. Everybody goes.' Tears welled in her eyes. 'I mean, I'm OK, I just need to talk. I was so scared.'

Therese handed her a tissue and held it as she blew her nose. 'You're safe now. We can help you here.' She moved the tray and sat herself on the bed. 'Where did you begin your trek?'

'I live on a farm in a valley overlooking the Kvænangen fjord, near Burfjord. I walked from there.'

'That's a long way away. Was your trek for recreation.' She

paused. 'Anna, are you OK?'

'I found a goblet on the ice, but that is lost now.'

'Anna, we do have a doctor amongst the guests. I could ask her to see you.'

Anna gripped Therese's arm. A deep breath shuddered out of her and left her face pained. 'I walked across the glacier to look for my husband. He disappeared three years ago. Emil Gironde. A photographer.'

'Did he come here?'

'I don't know. He was walking in the area. He might have gone anywhere.'

Therese considered the information. 'I can look in our albums, and the guest book, if that would help.

Anna nodded. 'More than ever I just need to know something about him.'

Therese got up. 'I will go and find out what I can.' She stood at the door. 'Next time I'll bring some serious chocolate cake, and some fresh clothes.'

When Therese had left, Anna ate the food on the tray, and then lay back and fell asleep. In her dream, she was looking through the photos on Kristin's camera. She looked specifically for the one Kristin had taken at arm's length, when she, Lars and Anna had smiled into the lens. Anna found the photo, remembered the smile she had pulled, but Lars and Kristin were not there.

When she awoke, Anna looked up at the ceiling and thought about what to do. She had made it to Uektefjord the hard way. If she had taken the easy route by boat, she would have never met Tomas in the hiking hut and learned about the villa. On the other hand, Lars and Kristin would not have been imperilled. Knowledge of the villa and the possibility that Emil would have liked it here seemed little reward for the effort.

There were people outside. She stood up, sore all over and stood looking out of the window. The beach shone like a strip of golden light. Warm air gusted upt to her. Begone Boreas and be replaced by the autumn wind; the season is not over yet. She took a shower, keeping her gloved hand dry outside the curtain. Wrapped in two towels from the bathroom, and then the bedspread, she realised that her clothes were a filthy mess. She wondered what to do when there was a knock at the door.

CHAPTER 31

'Come in,' called Anna. A pretty girl of six or seven in a yellow dress followed Therese into the room.

'This is my daughter, Alice.' The girl hid behind her mother's leg. Therese put down a tray with a teapot and a chocolate cake. 'Did you sleep well?'

'Yes, I did. Thank you.' She indicated the cake. 'You won't believe it, but the thought of chocolate cake kept me going.'

'Alice helped me make it.' The girl beamed at Anna.

Therese unwound the dressing and inspected Anna's hand. There were purple and orange bruises amongst the reddened skin. 'There is no exudate or blisters, which is a good sign. The swelling is going down. You must be quite fit and strong.'

'I survived, that is all I can say.' She startled. 'Lars. Kristin. Birgit.' What am I doing sitting here?' She started to get out of bed.

Therese calmed her down. 'Let me finish the dressing, or you will have problems.' When she had tended to the injured hand, she replaced Anna's glove.

'Kauppi, too, the glove is from the Sami. I must return it.'

'All in good time.' Therese placed slices of cake onto plates with spoons and handed one to Anna. 'Let's see what is happening outside today.'

They looked out of the window as they ate their cake. In the distance was a white ferry berthed at Oksfjord, a shining white hotel on bright blue water in front of dark blue mountains. Smaller boats made their way across the water to Uektefjord. When debarked, a steady line of passengers walked up from the quay, past the houses, and up to the villa.

'Look at those two old ladies, what pale faces they have,' said Therese. 'Alice, we know where they're from, don't' we?'

'England,' said Alice. 'Just like Sacha.'

Anna took the cup of tea offered by Therese. 'You have a lot of visitors, there must be a hundred or more.'

'Our assembly is getting popular. It always amazes me

when Martin's plan turns out so well. People come a long way to get here, from all around the world.'

Anna sipped the tea, which scalded her tongue. 'What about Berkeley? I've heard about him.'

'I'll you all about Berkeley. First, I'll get you some fresh clothes. Alice, do you want to ask Anna your question?'

Alice produced a hairbrush. 'Can I brush your hair?'

'Of course.' She moved so Alice could stand behind her and untangle her hair.

'You're doing a great job, Alice. Thank you. How do you like it here with all these visitors?'

'They're alright. People say Berkeley is a silly billy because he's not around much,' said Alice. 'I like Sacha the best'

'And who is this Sacha?'

'He's an artist. He paints pictures of us here, or the beach, or anywhere.'

Therese came back into the room with a pile of clothes for Anna. There was a long pair of dark grey trousers with many pockets, a man's checked shirt, a cream sweater, women's underwear and thick blue hiking socks with worn heels. 'This is the best I can do. Your own clothes will be washed and dried today.'

'This is so kind of you, Therese.'

'Not at all. There is some good news, too. I have a friend who works at the medical centre at Oskfjord. She confirmed that a teenage boy called Marco was taken there and treated for exposure. He recovered and was discharged yesterday, with no ill effects.' She smiled at Anna. 'You are a hero.'

'I don't feel like a hero. Thank goodness I was lucky to be there. Any news on my guides, Lars and Kristin?'

'My friend is checking. The glacier school hasn't replied.'

'Lars was bitten by the wolf. There might have been a serious infection. Kristin was not well.' Her voice trailed away. Alice stopped brushing her hair.

Therese held Anna's good hand. 'The glacier guides are not weak-willed creatures who collapse at the first hurdle. You survived, and I am sure that they did their best to survive.' Anna accepted some tissues from Therese. 'Didn't you say you killed a wolf?'

'Yes, I did.'

'How?'

'With a hammer.'

'I will book you as my guide the next time I go on a hike. Now, what did Emil look like? Do you have a photo?'

Anna pointed to her walking jacket. 'There is a photo in the inside pocket.'

Therese took out the photograph of Emil. 'A handsome man. I will show the photo to Martin and some of the others. Do you think he ever came here?'

'I don't know.' The tears began to form again. 'I don't know anything. I have lost everything.' She dabbed her eyes with fresh tissues. She startled again. 'Birgit!'

'You mentioned that name earlier. Who is she?'

'My sister. I told her I was searching for Emil. She will be worried.'

Therese held out her phone. 'Please call her.'

Anna shook her head. 'Her number is in my phone. It's out of charge.'

Therese crossed to the bedside table and picked up the phone. 'I will charge your phone. We have all the chargers ever invented.' She packed the tray ready to leave. 'What is this?' A red drop lay on the floor.

Anna picked it up. 'My necklace!' She searched through her clothes. Alice and Therese joined her on the floor looking for any more of the necklace. 'It was from Emil, an anniversary present, not that he lived to give it to me.'

'Alice, it's time to go now.' She held up Anna's phone. 'I will go and get this charged for you. You need to rest and let your hand heal up. Come down for lunch if you feel able. I will be up later to see how you are doing.'

Therese and Alice left Anna lying on the bed with her face covered by pillows.

CHAPTER 32

Anna rested until the evening. She held the solitary red tear in her hand and turned it over and over, watching the light glint on the glass. The imaginary rope bridge between her and Emil vibrated like a violin string. How had she fooled herself to think he was still alive? He was dead. Lars and Kristin were probably dead too, all because of her. And now she had lost the necklace, the final present Emil had bought her. She was, no doubt, considered a disgrace at home. She should have buried Gunnar properly or asked for help. She could have then gone to the pastor and arranged a memorial service for Emil. All this searching, where had it got her?

She lay and thought about the question. Her answer arose slowly, bravely, out of her situation. Searching had got her this far. Three years on she was finally confronting the problem head on. Therese or one of the visitors might know something. She looked at the men's clothes she wore. If she framed her hair just so, and somehow found a fake beard, perhaps she could act out Emil's part and jog someone's memory. There were more stones to turn over and she had to act now.

She stood up with aching back and legs. Her hand throbbed in the fur glove. She was alive. Birgit's phone number was in her phone, which she needed to retrieve from Therese. She closed the bedroom door with a click. There was no lock or key; perhaps the assembly had banished crime with the right form of words and an ethical attitude to people. A brown bear stood on the landing, in a glass cabinet, along with other stuffed animals and birds perched in the ceiling. This was a fascinating place. Emil would have come here if he had known about it.

A movement out of the corner of her eye turned her head, and she expected to see Emil standing in the doorway, just as he had done on his last day, waiting for a kiss, and for her to hand him his hat.

'Are you OK there?' a man said. He was about Anna's age, shorter, with tufted white hair and sideburns, and narrowed inquisitive eyes.

'Yes, I'm fine. My legs are a bit stiff that's all.'

'And you hurt your hand, I see. You must be Anna. Therese told me about you. I'm Martin.'

Anna waved the fur glove. 'Yes, I'm Anna.' She excused her appearance. 'I'm dressed in the clothes of at least two or three people. I must look a picture.'

'Can I help at all?' Martin wore a checked shirt, brown corduroy trousers, and a youthful smile on his face. 'Show you around?'

'I'm starving. I was hoping for something to eat, and to get my phone from Therese.'

'Follow me.' Martin led her downstairs then along a passageway. Outside the villa, through short and long windows as they walked, she saw a crowd of people with drinks in their hands sitting at tables under large blue umbrellas. Another crowd were on the beach, walking or paddling in the surf; someone was out in a rowing-boat. They walked past a mirror on the wall. She looked strange in the foreign clothes, the cream sweater too warm for the day. Her lips were cracked and bloody, her eyes with dark bags. This was her new self, after the blizzard, after her fight with the wind. And now she was here at Uektefjord, false fjord, at a place with other travellers who had been sensible enough to arrive by boat.

'Please come and have lunch with us.' Martin held open the door to a room lined with tables of food.

'I would like to pay,' she said. 'If you give me the details.'

Martin waved her request away. 'You are our guest. Please, have you what you like. I will be back in a moment.'

The tables boasted the best of her country's cuisine. Meatballs, salmon, cod, and a dish of brown meat she recognised as reindeer with a pot of juniper berry sauce and a pot of redcurrant jelly. Vegetables from the garden. There was caramel-coloured brunost; she thought of the milk she had left for Tuva to transform. On another table were bowls of raspberries and cloudberries. Would they have plums? Yes, of course; a bowl of the finest plums glistened in a white bowl.

She took a place at a table with the two old ladies she had seen walking to the hotel. Martin returned and placed her phone in front of her. 'We do have a land line that you are welcome to use, just ask Therese.'

'My thanks for your hospitality. The food is very good.'

'The villagers of Uektejford are used to us now, especially as we're quite a big employer in the area.' He winked and the two ladies opposite laughed.

'The friendly face of commerce, Martin, I am sure.' A hand extended across the table. 'Hello, my dear, I am Verity, and this is my sister Isabel.' Both sisters were in their sixties, Anna surmised, with hair in tight white curls.

'I'm Anna.'

'A local?' noticed Isabel.

'I live about a day's walk away; it takes longer in a blizzard and there is always the risk of frostbite.' She raised her fur glove and Verity and Isabel winced.

'You must be very brave.'

'Brave or foolish, the two are relations.' She looked at her table guests. 'What will you do today? I can let you know about places to visit.'

'We will meet old friends, and make new ones, talk, eat again of course, go for gentle walks on the beach, or up into the hills,' said Verity.

'But not all the way to the glacier,' said Isabel.

'I will not be doing that again. I was lucky to survive.'

'But mostly,' said Verity, 'we come here to relax, think, heal, discuss, unwind.'

'Or, as someone put it today, recharge,' said Martin.

'Recharge?'

'Draw sustenance. Bask in the light. Recharge, like a solar-powered battery.'

Anna nodded. Emil would have said the same thing. She so hoped that he had been here but there would be other times to ask.

Martin finished eating. 'Enjoy your stay with us, Anna. I must go now and give a talk on virtue ethics. After that I will drone on about stoicism, and what it means to be good. I will need the day off tomorrow.'

'He's a wonderful man,' said Isabel when Martin had left. 'Such an inspiration.'

'And Berkeley? Does he give talks here as well?'

'Oh, Berkeley is always late for these things.'

'Martin seems to do most of it,' said Verity.

Anna ate a fine meal and went to find Therese, who was in an office near the front door of the villa. Alice was drawing with crayons on paper. 'You look much better,' said Therese, 'rest up and you will be like new.' She handed Anna her phone.

There was a quiet room with a flickering fire where she was able to sit undisturbed. Birgit had called many times. At one point it seemed that her sister would call the police, then she saw a message reporting that she had been to the summer farm and Siegfried had explained everything.

'Birgit, it's me, Anna.'

'Takk Gud.' Anna heard footsteps running. Nina and Solveig crowded around the phone. She assured them that she was fine.

'Did you find Uncle Emil?'

'Nina, you idiot, be quiet,' said Solveig.

'No, Nina, I'm sorry. Uncle Emil wasn't to be found.'

Birgit picked up the conversation again and gradually calmed down once Anna convinced her that she was alright. 'We have been over to the farm,' said Birgit. 'Siegfried and Fridtjof were there. We are staying with Fridtjof.'

'Do I still own it?'

'You do.' Her sister laughed. 'Although they have many suggestions for the future. They say you should sell it, or lease it, or hire people to run it for you. We would love you to come and stay with us in Inari.'

'You know that I always think about that. The farm will not be the same without Gunnar, or Emil.' Anna explained where she was, accepting hospitality in a villa on the coast where the microclimate was mild and the food superb.

'Have you asked about Emil?'

'I have mentioned him to one person. I don't want to be the annoying guest at the party. I'm sure the news has got around about Emil, but everyone is very polite. I will make some enquires, as Inspector Rohde would say. They have treated me very well here, but I don't want to be a charity case.'

'How will you get home? Not walking again.'

'I'll figure it out. There are easier ways by boat, but then when did I ever do anything the easy way.'

'See if you can find out some more information about Emil. Somebody must know something.'

'Maybe, but most of the people here are foreign tourists, come to enjoy the company of like-minded people.' She touched her neck and missed the feel of the necklace. 'I even managed to lose the necklace Emil left me as a present. I only have one of the red tears and even that is damaged.'

'The necklace you found in the camera case?'

'Yes, I assume it was for me.'

'Of course, it was for you. It was intended as a surprise.' Her sister waited for the right time to say it. 'But that necklace is all in the past, Anna. It keeps you tied to the saddest moment of your life. Perhaps it is time to put the past aside and cry your last tear?'

She imagined that she was standing on the rope bridge with Emil, reaching out her hand to him. If I put the past aside, she thought, then the rope bridge falls away and Emil and I plummet to our deaths. People walked into the room, and when they saw she was talking earnestly on the phone, walked out again. People come and go, Anna mused. We are lent friends; we are lent lovers.

'Birgit, my dear sister, I don't often say this, but I think you are right.'

'Anna, I am lucky to be your sister. Come home safely to us.'

When she had resolved what to do, she walked along the beach, away from the boats that called in to the bay. The blue sea changed to green and the water foamed in the surf. Chunks of ice as tall as houses floated in the fjord. She listened to the glacier, further along the coast, calving, cracking, and rumbling, as pieces split off to form new icebergs that floated away in the distance, the light glancing off their jagged peaks.

Ice in the water over there, but here, she considered, dipping her good hand in the surf, the water is warm and clean.

She took out the red tear and turned it over in her hand for the last time. You never gave this to me, my love, but I know it was meant for me. She drew back her arm. It would do her good to be free again, free of the impossible past.

Emil, I don't want to do this, but I must. She threw her arm forward and opened her hand. The red teardrop flew up into the sky and splashed down in the sea. She stood watching the spot where the tear vanished into the saltwater.

CHAPTER 33

Alexander watched Anna throw something into the sea. The widow who had walked across the glacier in search of her missing husband. He approached her and hoped that he would meet someone as dedicated one day. 'Hello.' His greeting surprised her. 'I'm Sacha.'

He held out a brown paper bag filled with dried figs and dates. 'In secret anticipation of an Apollonian paradise.' he said, 'fruits of the harvest from Thessaly.'

She took a date from the bag. 'A journalist called Tomas told me that this place was called Hyperborea – a utopian paradise.'

Sacha nodded as he chewed a fig. 'Yes, Tomas was a lovely man. He wrote an article about us for his paper. But he never really got to the bottom of it what this place is for.' He pointed to where a stream bubbled up through the rocks.' They walked over and he scooped the water into his mouth. 'A gift from Apollo.'

She took her turn and drank the perfect water.

'Therese told me about the reason for your visit. I'm sorry to hear about your husband. What was his name?'

'Emil Gironde. He was a photographer.'

Sacha's face lit up. 'Gironde! I've heard of him. He did landscapes, deserted, isolated buildings, lots of sunsets, primary colour combinations.'

Anna was suddenly excited. 'Did you ever meet him? Did he ever come here?' She dug his photo out of her pocket.

Sacha shook his head. 'I know him from magazines. I think we have some in the villa, in the gallery. Sorry to say that I never met the man, never even knew he was a local, which is a shame. Believe me I would have liked that.' He looked at her disappointed face. 'I'm sorry.'

'It's OK. I'm getting used to the idea that he's gone. It's taken me a few years.'

They walked for a while along the beach into a warm

breeze. A structure became apparent on the sand: two pillars each made of flat tiles piled on one another. The horizontal beam was similarly built with brown tiles stuck together with a light clay. Anna did not go any further. In front of the doorway were two stone balls, one sphere larger than the other. On the other side of the doorway was the sea.

'What on earth is this?'

'Whatever you'd like it to be.'

'You sound just like Emil.' She looked up at the horizontal beam at the top of the doorway. 'Is it safe?'

'Completely, come wind or high water.'

Anna took a breath: it will take me two steps to walk through and yet I hesitate. Is there nothing in the world I do not fear? What do I have to lose? She squeezed between the two rocks, closed her eyes, and stepped through the doorway, ducking her head, lunging at the end to get away from the stones. She stood in the surf, the water lapping at her boots.

She turned and looked back at the doorway. 'Where did I pass through to?'

'The rest of your life.' Sacha walked around the doorway to join her.

'Hey, you didn't go through.'

'I've been through the doorway once before. There is no need to go through again.'

She followed him as she walked up the beach. 'What else have you made around here? Did you make the giant man in the mountains?'

He nodded. 'The humble giant. One of my favourites, and one of my first attempts at such a work. I'm quite attached to it. Took an age to get it up there on rollers, and now I hear it fell over in the storm.' He offered more dried fruit from the bag, which she declined.

'I had quite a shock when I saw the giant. Like he was watching me.'

'Others see the giant as helpful, others see it as malevolent in some way. That's people for you.'

'And what else have you made?' asked Anna.

'A shelter shaped like a ship's funnel. It was quite easy, just bricklaying, although it was a lot of bricks. The Sami helped with that one.'

'My guides called it the observatory. It was a welcome refuge in the storm.'

'You were with someone else?'

'A young married couple, Lars and Kristin. They got lost in the blizzard. I'm waiting to hear from them.' She looked down at her phone, but still there was no call or message from the glacier school. 'Everything I touch seems to turn to dust: Emil, Lars, Kristin, even my dog, Gunnar.'

Sacha shrugged and held up his hands. 'Just to let you know a secret.' He looked around the deserted beach. 'No-one gets out of here alive.'

Something ran up to Sacha in the white sand: a dark green and bronze lizard, its body thick and rectangular. Many more lizards joined in the inspection of the newcomers with slowly blinking eyes. 'Is this possible?' She asked. 'Lizards in Norway?

'A wise woman proportions her belief to the evidence.'

'Am I a wise woman?'

'You killed a wolf, survived a blizzard, and Therese says you will survive the frostbite. You've got something going for you.'

They walked along the beach. The tide had gone out and it was an easy walk over the wet sand. 'You obviously have a strong connection with your husband. It's impressive that you mourn in this way. In some countries, you would be wearing black, in memory of a man lost at sea.'

'There are men who would want me to do that in this country.'

One of the lizards, with the faintest suggestion of a yellow line down its spine, hopped towards them. With its large mouth and long head, it looked like it was almost smiling. The small animal jumped onto Anna's arm where it was content to sit. Other lizards appeared, and made short darting runs towards her. Some people wonder if there is an afterlife, she thought, but no-one imagines tame lizards waiting for them.

'It's like we're the first ones here, but of course we are not.'

They watched as a red crab dug itself a hole in the silky

white beach. Periodically, the crab popped up from its hole with more sand, until it suddenly departed, and they were able to look deep into the dark funnel of the animal's home and admire its industry.

Sacha returned the pet lizard to the sand. He sat down on a rock and let the lizards approach, feeding the bravest of them some grapes. They listened to the sea quietly lapping on the shore. The dark heads of small ice floes rose a few hundred yards out, and occasionally ice fell with a creaking crash into the Arctic Ocean. After a while, the warm breeze faded.

The light turned red: the clouds deepened to pink, the sky became washed with a curious yellow. 'Over there is Oksfjord. You can see the Hurtigruten ferry in the distance. It is possible to walk the entire way there along the coast, or take a small boat.' They made an about turn and walked back to the villa, paddling in the foam that curled up around their feet. Sacha produced a torch to light the way around the doorway when they reached it.

The villa glowed in the evening light: whites and silvers, hints of pastel blue and yellow along its pillars and arches. Its intricate design was cast in wood, but in parts it appeared to be sculpted from stone. There was the happy sound of a crowd outside on the deck around the dining room. Therese appeared at the door. 'Come in now if you want dinner.'

Anna was hungry and went inside. Sacha declined dinner, saying he was tired, and had eaten enough dried fruits to last him a day. Therese came out and gave him a hug and a social kiss. 'You're getting thin again.' She handed him a box of pills that Anna was not meant to see.

CHAPTER 34

In the morning, Anna went down to the dining room where she joined Verity and Isabel for breakfast. They wanted a blow by blow account of her trek and were amazed and impressed at every turn.

'To strive, to seek,' said Verity.

'To find nothing, and not to yield,' said Isabel, 'sorry, I don't mean to be insensitive.'

'Not at all.' Anna laughed. 'Beware the chilly Hyperboreans.'

Then Verity and Isabel told her about Martin's gallery which Emil would have liked if he had ever visited. 'Paintings, photographs, all sorts of art.'

Later, after meeting Therese and Alice for a walk on the beach, she found Martin in the gallery. He was hanging a new painting, of a brown rowing boat adrift without oars on a foaming green sea. On the seat where the absent rower would have sat, there stood a white candle in a silver nightstand. The yellow flame vitalised the picture.

'Do you like it?' asked Martin.

'It's straightforward. The lonely rowing boat, the person without direction, who is not even in the scene, who is lost at sea, letting the light shine the way, to end up where the fates will have it.'

'Yes, that's a reasonable interpretation as any. I would add that it was useful in describing part of a journey towards happiness.'

'Is this from one of your patients, or what do you call them, clients?'

'No, not from a client, or an analysand. You've met him, I think, while you've been here.'

'Do you mean Sacha?'

'Correct. He's our artist in residence.' Martin smiled. 'A proper paid job.' He whispered. 'You never know which gov-

165

ernment agency is listening.' He stood up close to the painting. 'Sacha produced this shortly after he came here. He had been through a lot by then, and some of his story he will never tell.' Martin stepped back. 'Or it could simply be a rowing boat on stormy seas.'

Anna looked at the painting again. It was out of place in a gallery full of landscapes, seascapes, the mountains, all of which were much better. 'I doubt if there is anything simple about Sacha. He is trying to find something. Emil would have called him a striver.'

'Now, I like this one very much,' said Martin, standing by a second painting on the wall. 'The land of snow and ice dotted with a few people, always convergent on the horizon.'

Anna stared at the painting and felt the icy breath of Boreas on her neck. 'It's just like being in a blizzard. You have no idea where you are, yet you try and keep moving.'

Martin nodded. 'And you survived, with the chance to start again.'

Anna flexed her injured hand, which felt better today. The backs of her legs were not so sore. 'Yes, I survived to tell the tale. I must thank Kauppi in person.'

They sat down on a bench and Martin let her talk about how Emil would have enjoyed visiting this place, the villa, the assembly. He would have loved to have met Sacha, but it seemed that Sacha arrived as Emil left the world.

'I buried my head in the sand. Waited for others to find him. Waited for him to come home. We trusted each other completely, loved each other totally. I knew that he hadn't left me.'

She looked around the gallery, at the images on the white walls. Silent conversations with the viewer, as Emil would have had it. The thought of turning the summer farm into a gallery in his honour came to her.

'Do you have any old photographs of previous meetings?'

'Therese keeps all the photographs. We keep nothing official, but she likes to take plenty.' Martin paused to let her go on.

'I would like to see if Emil came here. Maybe one of your guests met him?'

'Of course, that is a possibility.'

'I realise that it is a long shot.'

'You are looking for the last piece of this jigsaw puzzle, and you may or may not find it.' He brightened. 'Alice lost a piece from a jigsaw the other day. We looked everywhere. In the end we cut out the missing shape out of cardboard and drew on the part of the picture that was missing. It was as good a solution as we could think of.'

'You would like me to do the same for Emil? Complete my story without him?'

They looked out of the gallery window at the sea. The Hurtigruten ferry was crossing the horizon.

'I will write a letter to Emil, a last love letter. Yes, I will give it to a friend, Siegfried, he's our postman. He will take it to the post office in Burfjord.' She laughed. 'The letter will come back to me, delivered by Siegfried, who collects the mail from Burfjord every day. He will understand. I will place the letter, unopened, on the windowsill for Emil to read, next to his candle.'

Martin was smiling. 'And what will the letter say?'

'I will tell Emil that I've missed him greatly. I will tell him that I've not done well since he's been gone. I fear death, and the whole thing about dying. I fear abandonment. I pushed people away who tried to help me, including my sister and her girls. It's as if I am responsible for why Emil has gone. Perhaps that's why I was so fond of Gunnar and kept him so close to me. I thought that he would never leave me, but then he left and died.'

Martin straightened a painting. 'You put a lot of emphasis on the end. How about the middle bit, the doing, the living?'

Anna stood up and felt the strength in her legs. She smelt the preservative in the wooden benches, the leather on the seats. 'Earlier today I went out on the beach with Therese and Alice. I saw myself in Alice as she played out there, rushing in and out of the sea. The exhilaration, the excitement, the joy on her face, even when she ended up getting soaked.'

Anna looked again at Sacha's painting of the boat on stormy seas. 'I will write in my letter to Emil about my plans for the future. I will turn the farm into a gallery in honour of Emil.

Then I will move in with Birgit, and my nieces.'

Martin bowed his head ever so slightly.

Anna was about to leave the gallery when she caught sight of a large painting of an ice cavern. 'This is beautiful.'

'Sacha, again. One of his early ones. He absolutely refuses to use a camera.'

'He's the opposite of Emil, then. It was always photography with him.'

She studied the painting. 'Is that an eagle?'

Martin stood next to her. 'It looks like one. A freak of nature, literally, formed from the ice.'

Anna took a photo of the painting on her phone. She left the gallery and walked down the front stairs to the window with the best view out over the garden and beach. There were people on the sand and in small boats on the sea. Her senses were alive to all the smells of the building, of the aromas from the dining room, of fragrances from those she passed. As she walked upstairs she admired the solidity of the wooden banister that she gripped. She realised that she would not write a last letter to Emil at all; she had already sent it to him. She was in the future now.

Back in her room, she changed her dressing and was relieved to see the black bruises shrinking away. She lay on the bed thinking what to do next. The painting of the ice cavern by Sacha had caught her attention. Kauppi might know about it. She drifted off to sleep dreaming about another trip out over the ice.

CHAPTER 35

Voices drifted up to her through the open window. She realised it was afternoon. The veranda was filling up with people eating lunch. She felt much better, her legs and back relaxed, and her wounded hand was back to normal. Outside, the sea was flinty grey, and the light hazy with the sun low on the horizon. She went downstairs and joined the queue of diners.

After she had eaten, she found Therese outside, lounging in a chair on a private terrace. 'Come and join me. Alice is away with friends, and I have a rare moment of peace.' She looked tired with lidded eyes.

Chardonnay shone apple-green in a wine bottle half-full. Therese poured a glass for Anna, who waved her hand over the offering. 'I shall be straight to sleep.' Anna took in her perfume. 'Is that coconut?'

Therese nodded. 'Coconut soap. Do you like it?'

'It's lovely, especially out here, a coconut tree in the cold.'

'I'll get you some.'

'You're just too kind to me.'

Therese shrugged. 'Kindness is nothing. It's like breathing.' She took a sip of wine. 'Are you enjoying yourself here?'

'I do like it. I like the feeling of belonging among these people. I really like Verity and Isabel.'

'Those two ladies are wonderful.'

'I suppose I should go to some of the talks.'

Therese shook her head. 'You can if you wish, but it's not required, or even expected.' She lowered her voice. 'Martin much prefers it if people work things out for themselves. Not come and listen for answers.'

'He likes to talk.'

Therese's eyes opened wide with amusement. 'He could talk the hind leg off a reindeer. He's a professional listener.'

'He was helpful. I learnt something on my journey here.

169

Life is fragile, it's easily snuffed out, or whisked away. If Emil were alive, he would have been in touch. I have been foolish.'

The two women sat silent a while.

'You still wear your ring,' said Therese. 'I threw mine down the toilet the moment I knew my husband had cheated on me.'

'But you also wear a ring,' she said, pointing to Therese's left hand. 'From Martin?'

'No, we're not married. Elise turned the ring on her finger. 'This is just a cheap thing I found in a junk shop. Before our visitors arrived, I waited tables in a restaurant in the village. The ring keeps unwanted men away. They think I'm married, so they don't try so hard.'

'It's different for me. I'm flattered by the attention.'

'So, you have moved on.'

'No, I couldn't, I mean I never did. I could never have done that.' She thought about the future. 'It will be very weird now that I have let Emil go.'

Therese tugged hard at the ring on her finger, and let it spin on the tabletop. 'Even this reminds me of him, the man who left me with his child.'

'Martin appears to be a good father figure.'

'He is an excellent one, and his first time at it. But we've broken up twice, although we always seem to get back together. Perhaps we're pieces of the same pot. He's a good father to Alice. He says he'd like a son, but he's worried he's too old.'

'Who's Alice's father?'

'A man from yesteryear, gone and forgotten. Alice barely saw him, it doesn't matter. I was in Oslo for a while, scraping by, relying on friends. My uncle found me a job here. I painted, I waited tables, I got through the day. Then I met Martin.' Therese scratched the skin on the underside of her arms. Her skin was white, almost ivory, and where she scratched red dots sprang up.

'Men, always it's about men, the benefactors. Men take the drinks I offer, and pass their eyes over my body, seeing what else is on show.' She tossed back her hair and Anna was reminded of her fine figure. 'I'm the size I was before Alice. It's easy to diet. Drink a cup full of water before every meal and you eat less.'

Anna reached out and held her hand. 'You're doing well here, Therese. You have a new life, you're a good person.'

'But every few months we're off somewhere else, Martin spreading the word. I long to settle down in a village like this, or up on the hills or even in a town. Oh, listen to me. If I talk about myself for too long, I end up depressed.'

Anna said: 'Why don't you take off that ring, and have some fun?'

Therese smirked. 'I have all the fun I need.' She drained her wineglass. 'I should be looking out photographs for you, shouldn't I?'

'If you have time. Martin suggested you might have some photographs of your meetings here, around the time when Emil disappeared.' She took the photo, crumpled and dog-eared, of Emil out of her pocket. 'This was Emil a few years ago.'

'Keep it, I will get the albums out and we will look through them together.

Alice came weaving towards them through the tables. The girl wore a yellow and white checked dress with a yellow cardigan. Her hair was tied into pigtails with yellow ribbons. A pair of ballet shoes rode, tied together, on her shoulder.

Therese hugged her. 'Hello, baby, did you have fun?'

'I've been dancing,' Alice told Anna.

'There's dancing here?'

'In the next village, at Oksfjord,' said Therese. 'It's ballet, but at the end there's a disco. It's a life-saver.'

They talked a while longer then Anna returned to her room. The ice cavern, Kauppi, old photographs: she had a plan to follow. Inspector Rohde: I am following up on fresh leads.

There was a soft knocking on the door. 'Anna, it's me, Therese. I have the glacier school on the phone.' Anna opened the door and Therese gave her the phone.

A familiar voice greeted her. 'Anna! It's Kristin.'

Anna sat down on the bed. She recalled what it was to share body heat with her guides in the big orange bag.

'Kristin, are you OK? How is Lars, is he alright?'

Kristin started to talk but her voice rose as the tears came and she could not speak for a while. Anna waited.

'Anna, I'm so sorry. The cold got to me. Lars is at the medical centre in Oksfjord. The wolf bite left an infection. He's on antibiotics. How are you doing? You made it to the villa.'

'The Sami rescued me, a man called Kauppi. I had frostbite on my hand but that has been treated and I'm alright now.'

Her abandonment by her guides sat between them blocking the line. 'I'm glad you are both still with us. The storm was very bad.'

'Anna, I got so scared, I was so ill, I thought I was going to die. I had to find a better place to shelter. Lars came after me, but his leg was so bad he couldn't even walk on it. I found a track down to the coast and a group of Sami herders. They went back up for Lars and he told them where you were. Thank God they found you. I know we left you, that was my fault, please forgive me, I just had to get away.'

'Kristin.'

'Yes, Anna?'

'You saved us all, I can see that now. You were the one who found help.'

'Thank you, Anna. I was so lucky the Sami were there. I must go now. When Lars is better, we will meet again.'

'Kristin. Wait. Do you know anything about a large ice cave, so big you would call it a cavern?'

Kristin was talking with someone else. 'Anna,' she said. 'I have not seen it, but another guide has heard of a set of large ice caves in the region.'

'Where are these caves?' Anna waited for Kristin's reply, gripping the phone hard.

There was more talking in the background then Kristin was back. 'The manager says to try the hills overlooking Langfjordhamn. It is rocky terrain and he thinks there were some large ice caves over there once.'

'Has your colleague been there?'

'No, but he has heard stories. Anna, please remember this was a few years ago and you know the landscape is changing. I don't want you to be disappointed again.'

'I am beyond disappointment, Kristin. We will meet again for hot chocolate. Tell Lars that Nansen says hello.' She ended the call.

'Any luck?' asked Therese. She studied Anna's face. 'You've had some good news.'

'My guides are safe, thank goodness. Lars survived but he is in hospital with an infected leg. Kristin is alright. She was so scared in the blizzard she ran away straight into the Sami. One of her colleagues remembers some large ice caves from years ago in the hills near Langfjordhamn. I know the region, it is northwest of my farm. Emil could have easily gone there.'

'Maybe. It is only a small village. Is there really anything in those hills? It is remote country, nothing to see, and not on the way to anywhere.'

'It is on the road to nowhere.' She smiled at Therese. 'Emil would have loved it.'

'If you want to go there, you could take a boat from here to Bergsfjord and then south down the fjord to Langfjordhamn. Then hike up into the hills.'

Anna disagreed. 'Emil didn't take a boat. He was equipped to ski on the glacier. I must follow that route to have any chance of finding his path. That's why I started this dumb mission.'

'Then at least ask the Sami. They have snow cycles and quad bikes, like the one you arrived in. Kauppi is about, he will be sure to help you.'

Anna thought back to the freezing wind and blinding snow, about being ready to die in a crevasse. 'I do need some help. My trekking days are over.'

'I will ask Kauppi to take you to the hills around Langfjord-hamn. His herd has moved back inland now. You should also ask Sacha and see if he remembers the cavern. He has a studio further down the beach.'

Therese left Anna resting on the bed. For the first time in years she had a plan.

CHAPTER 36

It was quiet outside the villa, the building under a half-light that stretched across the sea. Dinner had been excellent. The good food had made a difference to her mood, keeping her hopeful. Her aches had become more diffuse, the bruises on her hand fading away.

Emil, she thought, looking out over the sea. You are why I am here. I made it here to find you, and if I am lucky, I will find your remains.

She walked over the glistening sand, through shells and seaweed, worm casts and pebbles, away from a boathouse she had discovered with Therese and Alice, away from the villa. Looking back at her footsteps on the sand, she had come a long way. Her route took her past the stone doorway, which she walked around, admiring the design, thinking about the foundations necessary to keep the structure in place despite the sea. There was a lot more to the sculpture than what appeared on the surface.

Around the curve of the bay, to where the sand stretched out along the coast to Oksfjord, she heard music. Up on the hillside was a small building with the statue of a man outside. The man was made up of inch-square silver, grey and brownish pixels. This could only be Sacha's studio.

The door to the two-storey building was closed, but not locked. Anna pushed open the door. The music was loud, the cones in unseen speakers buzzing against the casing. She rubbed the goose-bumps on her arms. It was cold in the room with the windows open in the far wall, the breeze clearing away the heavy smell of paints and white spirits. She recognised the music, the Petite Messe Solennelle by Rossini. It seemed as if a choir was inside the building, building up to some great announcement.

The ground floor studio was a long room. The furthest wall had been left as bare red bricks with a few occasional white bricks scattered throughout. Two windows, latticed in dark metal, were open. Sheets of paper fluttered in the breeze on a table filled with tubes of paint, pots of white spirit, stands of new and old brushes. A broad-tipped brush was still wet with brown paint. A metal bowl held a small white medicine pot with carbamazepine on the label.

By the table was an easel with a canvas, and on it fresh work, the rendition of a young calf reindeer. Half of the animal was reddish brown, thin legs, knobbly joints, flashes of white on its flank, leaf-shaped ears poked up expectantly, much as the animal would have appeared in nature. The other half was an abstract representation: a prism of brown, green and yellow shards. Sacha had transformed the dew on the grass into sparkling diamonds. En vakker skapning, she thought, a beautiful creature, caught outside the studio this morning, and made into a beautiful image.

Other paintings hung on the wall. There was the villa and its visitors. There was Martin, Therese and Alice. There was the coast with boats and large ships. There was the giant man holding his hands up to the sky. She remembered the small shelter it had provided her.

But it was the other white wall that intrigued her most. An enormous blue curtain, hung on a long horizontal pole, covered most of the space, too large to be a window. Golden cords hung by its side.

She looked around the studio. There were stairs leading up to the first floor. The music continued to play, rising to the preserved wooden beams of the ceiling. The choir seemed to want her to pull back the curtain, so she took hold of one of the golden cords and pulled.

She stood back in surprise and tried to take in the multi-coloured mural, stepping back into the middle of the room to look at the image in totality. The mural was a rectangle, twenty foot wide and ten foot high, an abstract mosaic of many colours. She had never seen anything like it; she waited until she could make sense of the information.

A few moments of looking confirmed the picture was abstract, made up of carefully placed shapes, not impressionistic points of paint. The image began to grow on her, and she began to like how the coloured shapes fitted together. The juxtaposition of scarlet, turquoise, indigo, tangerine, gun-metal grey and gold, seemed to follow a pattern, as if they were the result of a mathematical formula that placed each shape at the maximum distance from another shape of the same colour. Her brain worked hard to impose order on the chaos, and she began to see how two, or three, equivalently coloured shapes had been joined to make a meta-shape, and still these larger shapes did not disturb the overall pattern. She was pleased with this aspect of the image, and in wonder of its underlying order.

She allowed time for her brain to work out the strangely wonderful image, to understand the arrangement of the shapes, how each shape had four, five or six sides, but was surrounded by five, six or seven other shapes. There was a lot of information up close in the painting, so she backed away until she was up against the opposite wall, standing next to the reindeer, and trying to figure some sense from the abstract.

It is a woman's face, she thought initially, and then she settled on the idea.

A movement above her on the stairs caught her attention. Sacha dressed in jeans and a grubby tunic was standing on the balcony above the main room. He was staring at her. He had his hands raised out in front of him like he was sleep-walking. One leg was lifted over the balcony railing, seemingly ready to step over. He was swaying like a drunken giant on top of a tall tower.

'Sacha. What are you doing?'

'I can see the lights again.' He stared straight ahead at the two windows in the far wall, leaning the weight of his body against the balcony rail.

'What lights?'

'There are flashing blue lights outside.' He reached out to the windows. She turned to follow his gaze.

'They are floating, like blue spheres, the size of my hand.'

Outside the sea was calm and the sky was grey. 'There's nothing there, Sacha.' She looked up at him and started to walk over. He was pressing hard on the balcony rail.

'The blue lights are dancing. They are hitting the window,

like hard snow, like hailstones.'

'Is it the music? Are the lights part of the music?' She reached the bottom of the stairs, where she looked up and saw how he was balanced on the balcony. 'Can you paint the lights? The painting of the reindeer was lovely.'

Rossini's mass continued to rise, and she saw that Sacha was trying to follow the music into the air.

'Tell me about the lights, what are they doing now?' She started up the stairs slowly.

'The lights are bubbling up on the glass, chipping against the window in time with the music. Now, the music is softer, and the lights have settled down together, like baubles on a Christmas tree.'

She was halfway up the stairs. Sacha was halfway over the balcony, ten feet above the studio floor.

'You are an amazing artist. The woman in the painting. Who is she?'

Sacha's face dimmed. He began to mumble.

'It's a wonderful painting. At first, I thought there were two images, but I can see that there is one. It's a wonderful likeness when you see it.' Slowly she moved closer to him.

The look on Sacha's face changed. He began peering out over the balcony, staring at the abstract. With one hand he traced an image in the air as if he were the conductor of the voices and the beautiful piano. He leaned forward to get a fuller view of his work. The balcony rail cracked but did not give way.

'Is it a movie star?' she asked, almost within touching distance. 'Or someone classical, a Greek heroine, maybe, fitting for this place?' She kept her voice light as she inched closer to him and touched him with her fingertip.

His face dropped. The balcony rail gave way. His body fell forward, but she caught him as he fell. She pulled him back from the balcony and helped him lie on the floor, where he spasmed and hit his head on the doorframe to the bedroom. He banged his head again as he lost control of his muscles.

He moaned as he convulsed and thrashed about. She let him bang his head on her arms, ignoring the pain as he hit against it again and again. He cracked his elbow against the doorframe. Blood appeared on his arm and her hands. Spittle formed at his mouth and she was worried that he would bite his tongue. His face was red and the fire in his body transmitted through to her.

In the end, he lay exhausted and still.

'It's all right,' she said. 'You'll be OK. I'll get some help.'

He lay quietly on the floor, his eyes closed, chest rising and falling.

Anna whispered in his ear. 'Your art is wonderful. But you need a doctor.'

She stayed with him until he fell asleep. There was a bruise growing on the side of his head, some blood collecting around his ear. He remained still and she went into the bedroom and turned off the music. The poor man, she thought. She took the duvet off the bed and packed it between his resting body and the balcony. She heard voices outside, people on the beach who would come and help.

The light dimmed in the room as a cloud passed over. When she looked at the abstract on the wall again, she could see the woman was Therese.

CHAPTER 37

Martin followed Anna upstairs to where Sacha was lying outside his bedroom. 'Help is on the way.' He placed his hand on Sacha's head and smoothed his hair. There was blood on his fingers. Anna folded a pillowcase from the bedroom and pressed it against the wound.

Sacha raised his head a little. 'I've gone and done it this time.' He lay back. 'Now the rest of my life can begin.'

A petite woman in her forties arrived. 'This is Marie, she is a doctor.' The doctor inspected Sacha's head. 'There is swelling around the temple. He will need treatment at the medical centre.' She looked at his hands. 'I see that he has been painting.'

'A team from the medical centre is on the way,' said Martin, who stood up to let Therese through.

'Sacha?' she cried. 'Oh, no, not Sacha.'

Anna stopped her pressing across the balcony rail. 'Be careful here. The rail is not safe. Sacha nearly fell. He was climbing on the balcony and then he had a fit, a seizure. I tried to protect him, but he hit head on the door frame.'

The doctor looked at her. 'You were visiting him here? You were with him when this happened?'

'I came to see him to ask him about a place I wanted to visit. When I came in there was loud music playing. I had a look at his paintings, then I saw him on the balcony about to step over. I don't think he knew what he was doing.'

The doctor was looking into Sacha's eyes, and asking him to follow her finger. She pinched the back of his hand; he flinched. 'Sacha, do you think you had a fit? Do you remember?' He closed his eyes and turned his head away.

The doctor led Martin and Anna downstairs. Therese remained by Sacha's side talking softly to him. 'What do we know about this gentleman? Does he take alcohol, drugs? Is he on medication?'

Martin shook his head. 'I've never seen him drink. Drugs, I

doubt it, not with a mind like his; he doesn't need stimulation or sedation. He just needs to be.'

'There was something,' said Anna. She crossed the room and brought back the pill bottle she had seen, and another one she found amongst the paints.

The doctor read the label on the bottles. 'Carbamazepine, first line for epilepsy.' She tried the lid on both bottles. 'Unopened. One is two months old.'

'Why would he not take his pills?' asked Anna.

Martin sighed. 'Because he doesn't believe he is sick. He is an artist, and artists need a special view of the world. Drugs, prescription or otherwise, would have spoiled that.'

'Have you seen this?' Anna brought them over to the multi-coloured abstract. She looked up to the balcony where Therese was with Sacha.

'Modern art. Is there meant to be a meaning in it, or is it all expression?' The doctor answered her phone. 'The medical team has landed. I will go out and see them.' She left Anna and Martin looking at the abstract.

'Sacha told me that he was working on something big, not only in size, but concept. This is the first time I've seen it.' Martin gazed at the multicoloured shapes.

'What did he say about this?' Each time she looked at the abstract, she could not shake the image of Therese's face.

'Sometimes he regarded his work as his own interpretation of the world, ideas from within him. Other times, he hinted that he was painting something from outside that only he could see, that he was painting aspects of the *imago dei*, the face of God, a conclusion that he didn't really like.'

Martin stepped back and stared at the painting. 'It's a mess of colour. An abstract. There's no sense to it.'

'Stand here, next to the wall.' Anna dragged away the table laden with paints and paper to make more space. 'It's easier to see from here.'

Martin stepped back. 'Why, it's Therese.' Slowly his expression changed. 'Oh, I see.'

'I'm sorry.'

'Sorry, don't be sorry. I should have known.'

Alice ran into the room. She saw Therese with Sacha and

was about to run up the stairs when Therese called to her to stay back. 'Sacha has had an accident, Alice. He needs to go to the medical centre.'

Martin led Alice away without a word as the doctor returned.

'Do you remember what happened to you?' the doctor asked Sacha. There was no response.

Anna stood at the bottom of the stairs looking up. She waved for the doctor to come back down. His secret is out, she thought, a medical problem and an affair.

'What is it?' asked the doctor.

'When I found him, Sacha looked sleepy like a happy drunk. He had been working on the large picture on the wall. I think he had finished it. At first, he was pleased, and then the more he looked at it, less so, until he got to the point when it didn't seem right to him at all.'

'His injuries are consistent with a violent fit. His medication is consistent with epilepsy.'

'Maybe it was all to do with the fit.' She didn't like to give away secrets, but she wanted the doctor to give him the right help. 'He said he saw blue lights flashing in the windows, in time to the music.'

'Visual disturbances are common in epilepsy. Falling asleep after seizures is common, as is no recall of the event. Thank you for this information. He will get good attention at Oksfjord but will have to go on to a larger hospital.'

'Martin will be able to help with that; he is his employer.'

Anna closed the windows now that the place was so cold. On the beach she saw a ridged inflatable boat. Two men in orange jackets pushed a stretcher on a trolley up the beach to the studio. The doctor met the paramedics at the door and they discussed the best way of getting Sacha down the stairs.

Anna looked again at the abstract. It was an amazing picture, the way he had put the colours together, the way he had built Therese's face so that it was only seen from a long way back.

Ten minutes later, the paramedics brought Sacha downstairs strapped on to the stretcher. The doctor followed them to the boat.

'There, you know about us now, Anna.' Therese sat on the lowest step and watched them go.

'It's only a painting, perhaps an infatuation.'

'Martin will never believe that, and it's not true, either. We loved each other.'

They went outside to join the crowd assembled outside the villa. Anna touched the pixellated man outside the studio. Made up of parts, ready to assemble or dissemble. One of the pixels was loose and she put it in her pocket.

She met Verity and Isabel who were watching the paramedics prepare to load the stretcher into the boat.

'The poor man,' said Verity. 'He was the artist here, although we didn't see much of him.'

'I liked some of his paintings,' said Isabel. 'I hope he will be OK. It is in the medics we trust, especially at our age.'

One of the paramedics was returning from the boat to the crowd. Martin met him, turned around and pointed at Anna. The paramedic came over. The badges on his jacket reminded her of Lars.

'Are you Anna?'

She nodded.

The patient wants to tell you something,' said the man. 'Please come quickly. We need to go.'

She followed the man to where Sacha waited on the stretcher, surf lapping at the wheels of the trolley. He tugged at her sleeve and his hand gripped the fabric of her shirt tightly. She leant down to listen to the words he was mouthing.

'Anna,' he whispered to her.

She felt his grip tighten.

'What is it?' she asked.

'The ice cave in my painting.' Then he coughed, and his eyes closed, and the paramedics became agitated.

'Yes, I want to go there and look for Emil. The glacier guides think it is near Langfjordhamn.'

She waited but there was nothing more from him. The paramedics started to lift Sacha into the boat. Then he opened his eyes and said with some effort: 'Due west of the Watcher.'

'The first giant man we saw? I remember him! Thank you, Sacha.'

The paramedics took over, hoisting the stretcher onto the boat. The outboard motor kicked up the surf and the boat reversed, swung around, and headed back to Oksfjord.

Anna followed the crowd back to the villa. Therese and Alice came up to her. 'What did he say?'

'There is an ice cave near Langfjordhamn. It is the one in the painting.'

'That's great news!'

She shrugged. 'Perhaps Emil went there, perhaps not.'

They watched the boat speed over the water to Oksfjord. The sun glowed across the horizon. A golden twilight persisted as the breeze grew colder and the sea turned dark and grey.

CHAPTER 38

N ew skis and a new backpack with food and water were found for Anna. The first part of her journey was to walk along the edge of the fjord and, once at the end, walk up the grassy hillside and onwards to join the arm of the glacier. Here she would meet Kauppi and another man, Isak.

She set off, mindful of the last time she went out for a walk, and the familiar feeling of searching for a needle in a haystack returned. Her only clues were circumstantial, based on the events of years ago, and the painting of a young man who saw things differently to those around him. She was relieved to meet Kauppi and Isak at the start of the glacier as planned. Kauppi put a ring of stones around her neck, whether good luck or a condolence she didn't ask. She sat behind him on a snow cycle. Isak rode the other machine.

They set off following well-worn ski tracks. Travel was easy through sparse forests of pine. She told Kauppi to head for the Watcher, and while he was not pleased about the prospect, as he disliked the idea of giant statues littering his homeland, he agreed in the end. They stopped to stretch their legs, and to drink water and eat plain flatbreads. When they reached ground made more difficult with rifts, ridges and crevasses, they stopped and put on skies. Isak would wait there for their call.

Kauppi led the way and Anna followed. He took her along a more sheltered route, one used for herding reindeer. She realised how exposed her route had been on the outward journey, always aiming for peaks and the scenic view to check bearings. Kauppi in contrast navigated by the trees in the lowlands.

It was late afternoon when they reached the Watcher. She skied up to the giant man with a grin on her face. Please be the waymarker who watches over Emil. She took out her compass and checked the bearing was due west. The land moved upwards in gentle rolls with sudden depressions, ridges and hollows and would be a test to her skiing. But she preferred that test over waiting for the weather to close and Boreas to reappear.

She took the lead and Kauppi followed. She kept west, checking the bearing every so often. Each time she stopped, Kauppi pointed their intended direction, and each time he was correct by her compass. His affirmation raised her spirits. After an hour they came to a choice of paths, one heading downhill on a route that looked well skied, the other way would require a trip on foot into rocky terrain.

Kauppi stood by her side and checked the compass bearing. 'There are many places to look.' He took out a pair of binoculars and handed them to her.

She surveyed the landscape and zeroed in on Langfjordhamn below. The village would be difficult to get to over rocky terrain, perfect for hiding ice caverns. 'I have looked everywhere,' she told Kauppi, 'I cannot stop now.'

Kauppi did not comment. It was her search. Perhaps the stones around her neck really were a condolence for a desperate widow paying her last respects to her.

She felt the familiar feeling of despair wash over her. She was in the middle of nowhere again, searching for someone who didn't exist. Hills of snow and ice lay in front of her, hiding their secrets. She looked harder, desperate for a clue. Sacha had painted inside the cavern; there had been no clues as to what was outside.

Snow was melting all around her, large chunks slipping off rocks, turning to slush on the ground. Kauppi moved ahead instinctively and she followed him, carefully scanning the scenery, not wanting to miss anything. Her compass bearing was due west. Trust Sacha, trust Kauppi, trust yourself in this game of hide. What she really wanted was for Nina and Solveig to appear suddenly and call out cold, or hot!

She was about to scream in her desperation for a clue, when she saw an archway built of snow and ice. The structure was tall enough for a person to fit underneath. She called Kauppi over. 'There is something here, part of something larger maybe.' They went through the archway and saw that it led up to the side of a hill.

Kauppi looked at the hillside with suspicion. He made a hole in the blank wall of snow with his gloved hand. The hole widened revealing a honeycomb structure of snow, ice and air. Anna joined him, using her good hand to scoop away the snow. She was suddenly through into a such a large space that she called out in surprise. 'It's a tunnel!'

The snow came tumbling away and together they made a space large enough to step through. Kauppi looked around in admiration of the long blue tunnel. The look on his face was all she needed to get her hopes up. He fixed a head torch over his hat and she did the same.

They walked down the tunnel, lighting up the glistening walls. Anna's hopes were sky high. This was it, it had to be. Then tunnel suddenly became narrower with each step, until finally she faced another white wall of snow. Anna scraped at the wall but it was no honeycomb; it was much firmer.

She kicked at the wall. 'Is this it?' she asked out loud. Is this really it? Is this it for me?' She took out her ice axe and sank it into the wall. The axe stayed where it was put and Kauppi had to pull it out. After minutes of hitting, kicking and slapping the wall, they admitted that there was no way through.

The evening was drawing in. Kauppi pulled out his phone and she saw a map with a blue dot giving their position. She checked her watch. It was time for the rendezvous with Isak and a decision: either a return to Uektefjord or hiking down to Langfjordhamn with Kauppi.

Both prospects would leave her empty-handed. There was nothing for her out here but more snow and ice. She must be the dumbest, most foolish person in the world. She sat back against the wall and waited for Kauppi to make the decision. Kauppi went back toward the archway to wait for Isak.

Inspector Rohde, I have tried my best. Three years on when the police found nothing, I also have found nothing. I remember the time in your office when you likened my search to that of scientists searching for some tiny part of the atom. You told me about the energy involved in those experiments, crashing atoms together, watching the debris fly out, calculating the probability that what you had found was the right piece of the jigsaw. You told me that the energy of the police force was used up on this case, that the probability of finding Emil was so low. So many missing people don't want to be found, and after a certain period of time, they are never found.

So why do I believe there is still something here?

She heard a snow cycle approaching in the distance. Isak was in the area ready to take her back. Or she might hike down on her own and throw herself off a cliff, if she were brave enough.

Kauppi came back down the tunnel and offered her his hand to get up. She took it and rose to her feet. They listened to the snow cycle moving around their location.

'Will he be able to find us?'

Kauppi shower her his phone. 'GPS. There are crossed skis outside to mark the place.'

The noise of the snow cycle grew louder then faded then grew louder again. Then there was silence which extended from seconds to minutes.

Kauppi was frowning at his phone which showed two blue dots at the same position.

Suddenly, there was a movement in the snow behind her. Kauppi pulled her back just as the blade of an ice axe appeared through the wall she had been sitting against. Gloved hands appeared next, and then a boot and a leg, thrust through the snow with a mighty kick. Finally, Isak crashed through the hole and landed in front of them.

Anna looked through the hole into a cave filled with sunlight.

'It's a cave! He fell into a cave!' She stepped into the hole and pulled herself through into the short tunnel Isak had made to get out.

Already she could see that the place was huge, full of dark shadows and patches of light. She saw the snow cycle on its side illuminated by light coming in the broken roof. There was the sound of dripping water suggesting hidden corners of the cave. She wanted to explore.

Kauppi emerged behind her. He put a hand on her shoulder. 'Isak says he found a body.'

Her head swam and Kauppi helped her stand upright. A

body, at last. She held on to Kauppi as she looked around the cavern.

'Is it Emil?'

'You must look over there.' Kauppi pointed to the furthest corner of the cave in the shadows.

She walked towards the shadows, her head torch lighting up the walls and floor of the cave. As she approached, she saw something that made her shrink back. Kauppi and Isak were behind her. She waited, eyes adjusting to the torch-lit gloom, until she could see what it was.

The body was sitting down, in a half-reclined position, as if trying to rise, legs bent at the knees, the implied motion one of upwards and onwards. Emil still had on his brown boots and blue trousers. His right boot was buried in the snow and ice. Snow covered his chest and the side of his body in feathered patterns. His left hand was bare, formed together into a fist. His right hand was in the pocket of his green jacket, hidden under the snow. His head was bald, a shade of brown that matched the rocks around him. His shirt had either ridden up, or had been torn, to reveal a naked orange-brown back. Frozen into the sitting position, she imagined Emil had been reaching forward, ready to stand, but had been stopped by injury and the cold.

She stepped closer with Kauppi by her side. 'Is this your husband?'

'Yes, it is Emil,' she whispered. 'Those are his clothes and boots. He's lost the hair on his head.' She put out her hand but drew it back. 'I want to touch him, but I can't.'

Anna stood looking at his body. Emil had fought until the cold had become unbearable. She inched slowly around the body until she could see his face. He was looking downwards, his eyes dark and his strangely coloured head fractured.

Isak took something from the damaged snowcycle and presented it to Anna. She recognised a garland of white flowers in her hands. Somehow, she managed to walk up to Emil's body and lay the tribute over him. The tears came and she could see no more.

Kauppi led her away to where she rested against the snow-cycle. 'Isak has gone to get help. We will stay here.'

CHAPTER 39

Anna took the boat with Siegfried who had come out to meet her at Uektefjord. They sped along the coast, weaving between peninsulas and islands, past bays with columns of rocks at their entrances, wild and remote, and quiet plains with lush green grass and sheep grazing. They passed inhabited villages, and abandoned communities of huts and cabins alike. At one location, nestled at the foot of a dramatic steep cliff that rose straight out of the sea, they saw a collection of decaying brown huts next to a lonely church and a small graveyard with a few headstones. Without upkeep the huts would be smashed to pieces by the elements, by the wind and rain, snow and sleet, and the grass would reclaim the churchyard.

At the island of Loppa they turned west and at the headland of Andsnes and Seglvik they headed south. Siegfried pointed up at an eagle holding station. Dolphins and porpoises rode alongside the boat. They rounded the coast and kept to the left of the islands, Radoy, then Splidra. The familiar white-capped mountains of Joeksfjord appeared ahead. Siegfried turned the boat north and they sailed up their home fjord. The summer farm appeared in the distance on the left. There were children out in the garden flying a kite.

She walked up the track and saw the dragon flying in the sky. A kite. Nina and Solveig were in the pasture. They were giving the kite a lot of string, letting it fly as high as it would go. The beast, a red dragon, threatened to run away with them. The kite flexed and snapped in the wind and rose above the land when they tried to catch it. The weather, once calm on the fjord as she came in from Kaevengnen, was now playful. The wind raised Anna's hair into peaks; you tried to kill me, Boreas, but I made it through. Birgit called out to Nina to be careful, that it might not be safe to play for too long. But Nina wanted to play, and her mother did not have the heart to stop her.

Nina lifted up the kite and offered it to the sky. The dragon bulged as it took in a giant gulp of air; its body stretched and struggled and tried to break away from the little girl's white hands.

Up into the sky shot the dragon, rising vertically above their heads, tugging on the lines that bound it to earth. Nina put on her orange sunglasses, so that she would not be blinded by the sun, and pulled hard on her line, forcing the dragon to turn in a circle. The dragon swooped above her, its long red body extending to its full length, its head and jaws searching for places to go.

Anna remembered flying a kite with her father. She reckoned she was Nina's age at the time. She remembered the pain as the strings wrapped around her hands, and her kite ran out of control. It was a pink kite, a flamingo, not a dragon, but it flew equally energetically up into the sky. Her father shouted to her to shorten the line, to wind the string onto the cradle, hold it close to her chest, but she did not have the strength, and nor did her father help her. Her mother watched from afar, from the kitchen window, anxious, but not allowed to interfere.

Anna squinted up at the sun and watched Nina's dragon licking the beach with flame. The dragon sailed on higher into the sky, laughing at the silly humans, and the higher it climbed, the more the dragon urged the girl hanging below to join it in the stars.

Anna remembered how she had got her fingers trapped between the line and the wooden cradle. The flamingo had squeezed with glee until she lost her footing and the bird went ballistic. But Anna had not been so easily dismayed. She skipped across the meadow, trying to keep up with the fluttering flamingo, and for seconds at a time her mother told her she was flying.

Somewhere in her daydream, Anna heard Nina call out and then scream. Nina was being dragged by the kite and blown by the wind towards the fence. Birgit shouted to Alice to drop the cradle, to let it join the one scuttling away from her across the grass. Anna watched. There may be injuries, people might be harmed, a new kite would be needed.

The wind picked up the kite and made it flap madly, like a bird at a window. Nina continued to chase the monster. The red dragon tugged and yanked on the line binding it to the girl, but she held on.

Then the dragon got angry. It saw the girl as a tasty meal, and so down it dived, strafing her in a melee of flapping plastic. Nina rolled away in a ball, holding on to her cradle. It was a fabulous fight. Nina never let go of her line and slowly she fought back, crawling across the beach to where the second cradle lay.

Birgit got there first and held on to the cradle. 'OK,' she said, 'I've got it now.'

The wind blew and the dragon jumped vertically for the moon. Birgit held on as she tamed the dragon. She slowly wound the line in on the cradle, lowering the dragon to the ground, until it ran out of wind and dived into the pasture. Anna walked over and put one foot on the flapping beast.

'Anna! You're home.' Birgit put some stones on the kite to hold it down. The two sisters embraced.

Anna picked Nina up, and held Solveig close to her when she ran up.

'What news?' said Birgit.

'Good news,' she said. 'I will tell you the story.'

They met in Anna's living room after tea in the kitchen. Fridtjof had put Birgit and the girls up at his farm again when he heard that Anna was on the way home.

Siegfried was in the rocking chair, looking like he owned the place. He held a cardboard tube. 'One last surprise from your husband,' he said.

Anna, sitting on the sofa with Fridtjof, laughed. 'I never even knew about this strange camera on our roof. I would have cleared it away.'

Siegfried produced the beer can and an explanation. 'It was a simple pinhole camera.' He pointed to a spot midway up the beer can. 'Inside was a piece of photographic film. All you need do is place the can to take in the view, uncover the hole, and leave the picture to expose for a month or more. Emil was lucky it stayed attached to the roof for so long.'

'And there is a photograph to see?'

'Oh, yes.'

'Did you develop it? Siegfried, you're amazing; you can turn your hand to anything.'

'No, I didn't do the work; I had some help' Siegfried indicated Emil's photography books on the shelf. 'I contacted one of his old photography clubs in Tromsø. They told me to come in and they would take care of it. I took the train into Tromsø. They thought I was some Nordlending who had got lost.'

There was laughter at Siegfried's story.

'I made up some story about it being my nephew's project, and he needed it for school, or his birthday was coming up. Anyway, they developed it.' He frowned. 'No that's not right. They didn't use chemicals. The woman who helped just took out the film and laid it flat inside in a scanner. They did that in the dark with a red light on. I had to wait outside.'

He took out a small piece of photographic film about three inches long. The image is on here. We made some hard copies on paper. Do you want to see them?'

'Of course.' They were all up out of their seats crowding around him.

Fridtjof asked: 'What did this cost you, old friend? A trip to the city, modern technology. I know you will tell me the real number.'

'Four thousand krone.'

'Herregud,' said Fridtjof. 'That is a meal in the best restaurant in Tromsø!'

'He is joking, of course,' said Anna. 'Whatever the bill is, I will pay it. Now, let us see the image.'

They all crowded around Siegfried as he took a roll of paper out of the tube. He laid out the photograph on the table using objects to keep the edges down. When they saw the photograph, they gasped. The fjord was dappled in blue and greens, and above it the sun traced multiple golden arcs across the pink-brown sky.

'It's beautiful, amazing.' Anna kissed Siegfried on the cheek.

'The lady who developed this said it was unusual to be such a good image after three years. I didn't tell her it was by a famous photographer.'

'I love these shining spots here.' Anna pointed to bright luminescent spots of blue on one side. 'Look in the sky, and then here on the edge of the photo.' She studied the image. 'Look, are these the goats? That is their favourite place, under the plum trees.' She was delighted. 'I will get it framed. Emil's last photo will look wonderful above the fireplace, in pride of place.'

Solveig was counting the solar tracks across the sky. 'Twenty-two paths of the sun,' she said. 'Some smudged but I like it.'

Fridtjof clapped Siegfried on the back. 'Well done, old friend!'

'Uncle Emil was the best!' said Nina.

Anna smiled. 'Yes, he was the best. I miss him terribly, but he is safe now.'

They ate dinner in the kitchen: roasted goat kid, flatbreads and brunost. Fridtjof produced a bottle of red wine. Siegfried feigned ignorance about the existence of anything stronger in his hip flask. Birgit stood and proposed a toast to Emil. Anna accepted the toast with shining eyes. Nina and Solveig were allowed a sip of wine, which they declared was disgusting. Their laughter echoed around the farm and up into the sky.

ACKNOWLEDGEMENT

Thank you to my wife, Lisa, and our children, Louis, and Emily, for time and space to write. Encouragement comes from many places; friends, fellow authors, good reviews; it all adds up and keeps me going.

Printed in Great Britain
by Amazon